ROOM ONE

ALSO BY ANDREW CLEMENTS

Lunch Money
The Last Holiday Concert
The Report Card
A Week in the Woods
The Jacket
The School Story
The Janitor's Boy
The Landry News
Frindle
Big Al
Jake Drake, Bully Buster
Jake Drake, Know-It-All
Jake Drake, Teacher's Pet
Jake Drake, Class Clown
Big Al and Shrimpy

Andrew Clements

Illustrations by Mark Elliott

Aladdin Paperbacks

New York · London · Toronto · Sydney

ALADDIN PAPERBACKS · An imprint of Simon & Schuster Children's Publishing Division · 1230 Avenue of the Americas, New York, NY 10020 · Text copyright © 2006 by Andrew Clements · Illustrations copyright © 2008 by Mark Elliott · All rights reserved, including the right of reproduction in whole or in part in any form. · ALADDIN PAPERBACKS and related logo are registered trademarks of Simon & Schuster, Inc. · Also available in a Simon & Schuster Books for Young Readers hardcover edition. · Designed by Greg Stadnyk and Jessica Sonkin. · The text of this book was set in Revival. · The illustrations were rendered in pencil. · Manufactured in the United States of America · First Aladdin Paperbacks edition May 2008 · 10 9 8 7 6 5

The Library of Congress has cataloged the hardcover edition as follows:

Clements, Andrew.

Room one : a mystery or two / Andrew Clements ; illustrations by Mark Elliott.

p. cm.

Summary: Ted Hammond, the only sixth grader in his small Nebraska town's one-room schoolhouse, searches for clues to the disappearance of a homeless family.

[1. Schools—Fiction. 2. City and town life—Fiction. 3. Homeless persons—Fiction. 4. Mystery and detective stories. 5. Schools—Juvenile fiction. 6. City and town life—Juvenile fiction. 7. Homeless persons—Juvenile fiction. 8. Nebraska—Fiction. 9. Nebraska—Juvenile fiction.]

PZ7.C59118 Ro 2006

[Fic] 22—lcac

2006004303

ISBN-13: 978-0-689-86686-9 (hc.)

ISBN-10: 0-689-86686-0 (hc.)

ISBN-13: 978-0-689-86687-6 (pbk.)

ISBN-10: 0-689-86687-9 (pbk.)

For my sister, Martha Clements Wilday

Chapter 1

MAY

Ted Hammond huffed and puffed as he pedaled up the small hill on the road back into town. Every morning he rode his bike to the junction of Route 92 and County Road 7 and picked up a bundle of the *Omaha World-Tribune*. And between seven thirty and eight thirty, rain or shine, summer or winter, Ted delivered the news.

The newspapers in his canvas shoulder bag felt like they weighed a hundred pounds. That's because it was Tuesday, and that meant he had an extra bundle of the county paper, the *Weekly Observer*. But at least there wasn't any snow or rain or hot dust blowing into his face.

May was Ted's favorite month for bike riding. Not too hot, not too cold. He loved October, too. But with May, summer wasn't far off, and summer meant no school. So May was the best.

It wasn't like Ted made a lot of money delivering papers, but in Plattsford, Nebraska, any job was a great job. Even during its high point in the 1920s, Plattsford had been a small town, not much more than a speck on the Great Plains of west central Nebraska. And for years and years the population had been shrinking.

But that didn't bother Ted. He liked the leftovers, the people who were still around. And when the Otis family had moved away? Didn't bother Ted a bit. He had delivered papers to them for two and a half years, and they'd never given him a tip, not even a dime—not even at Christmas. Plus Albert Otis had been a dirty rotten bully.

Good riddance.

Ted could ride up and down the streets and know who lived in every house—well, nearly. He didn't personally know all 108 people who lived in Plattsford, because the whole township covered thirty-six square miles. But the in-town part, the part where he had most of his paper route, that was only about forty houses, and he'd knocked on almost every door looking for new subscriptions or collecting money from his customers. His last stop every day was Clara's Diner, right on Main Street, and a homemade doughnut and a glass of milk was always waiting for him on the end of the counter.

With a last burst of effort, Ted got his bike over the crest of the hill, and then he was coasting down the other side, the early sun bright on his face. Bluebirds singing along the fence row, the waving grass beginning to green up, the faded red paint on the Andersons' barn—Ted pulled it all into his eyes and ears, and then into his heart. He loved this place, his own peaceful corner of the world.

And when Ted happened to see a face in an upstairs window of the Andersons' house, he wanted to smile and wave and shout, "Hey! Beautiful day, huh?" But he didn't. And there was a good reason for that. The Andersons had moved away almost two years ago, and the old farmhouse was empty, boarded up tight.

At least, it was supposed to be.

Chapter 2

THE SIXTH GRADER

When Ted got to school at nine o'clock, his day was almost three hours old. As he'd delivered his newspapers, and then munched his doughnut at Clara's Diner, there had been plenty of time to think about what he'd seen as he went riding past the Andersons' house.

Ted even asked himself if maybe he hadn't imagined it. But no. He was sure he'd seen a face, a girl's face. And she'd had brown hair that covered one cheek almost down to her chin. And she'd pulled back into the shadows just as he rode past and glanced her way. She hadn't wanted to be seen.

As curious as Ted was, there was nothing he could do about it, not until later. Not until after school. And he had a feeling it was going to be another long day. When the weather got beautiful, every school day lasted forever. Especially in room one.

There was an old joke, and it was supposed to be funny. Someone would ask, "Where should we have the school play?" And someone else would say, "I know! Let's use room one."

Or a kid would say, "Where can we have the spelling bee?" And another kid would say, "How about . . . room one?"

Or the scoutmaster would say, "I wonder where we should hold the big pancake breakfast this year?" And a boy would pretend to think real hard, and then offer, "Umm . . . room one, maybe?"

The person asking and the person answering were both in on the joke, because everyone in the town of Plattsford, Nebraska, knew that if you didn't count the bathrooms and the small front office, Red Prairie Learning Center was a one-room school. The one and only classroom was room one.

And in that one and only room, there was only one sixth grader, and that was Ted Hammond.

To call Red Prairie a one-room school wasn't completely correct, because the building actually had seven classrooms. As recently as fifteen years ago, there had been over a hundred children attending in grades kindergarten through five. Back then the town even had its own junior high school.

But as the local farms and businesses went through year after year of hard times, more and more families had moved away. Eight years earlier, the junior high school had closed, and the sixth, seventh, and eighth graders joined the younger kids at Red Prairie—which meant that some grades had needed to double up in the same classrooms.

As the number of students kept dropping, classrooms were shut down, no longer needed. The long fluorescent lightbulbs were removed from the ceiling fixtures to be used in other rooms. The heating and ventilation systems were turned off to save money. The custodian stopped sweeping the floors, and if a window in an empty classroom got broken, it was covered with plywood. Finally, only the large room near the front office was kept open, the room that had been used for assemblies and lunch—room one.

It was a good thing that room one was so large. There was enough space in the reading corner for the eight long bookshelves that had become the school library. There was enough space for three computer desks, except only two of the computers were working at the moment, and the dial-up Internet access was painfully slow. There was even enough space for a couple of foursquare courts near the center of the room, which were put to good use on indoor recess days.

Just two years ago, Red Prairie Elementary School had been renamed Red Prairie Learning Center, and this year there were only nine students in room one.

On the younger end there were four fourth graders: Lizzie, Hannah, Kevin, and Keith. On the older end, there were four eighth graders: Josh, Eddie, Carla, and Joan.

And smack dab in the middle, there was one sixth grader.

Was the only twelve-year-old in town a loner, friendless? Not Ted Hammond. There were two other sixth-grade boys who lived in Hulton, about twenty miles away. They were in his 4-H Club, and the meetings were every other week. The three guys had gone to the 4-H summer camp in Halsey last year. They weren't neighbors or classmates, but they were good friends just the same.

Ted also spent time working side by side with his dad around the farm, and the whole family ate dinner together every night. And delivering the newspapers kept Ted in touch with almost everyone else in town. There wasn't much time left over to feel lonely.

True, during the school day Ted was on his own a lot, and it would have been great to have one good friend. But did he miss having a big gang of kids his age? Not really. Ted's time at school was interesting in its own special way. It was almost restful. Almost boring, too—but only now and then.

Red Prairie Learning Center had a total population of ten people, if you counted the teacher. And, of course, you always have to count the teacher. Even though the total number of students was small, Mrs. Mitchell still had a big job with plenty of juggling. A few activities like art and music could include the whole group, but most of the time the three different grade levels needed individual attention. Mrs. Mitchell had to prepare the eighth graders for high school. She had to help the fourth graders with their reading and basic math. And she had to try to keep her one sixth grader from just sitting in a corner with a book all day.

Because that's what happened if the teacher didn't keep Ted focused on his math and social studies and language arts and science. Even during outdoor recess, Ted sometimes made up an excuse to go back into the room, and Mrs. Mitchell would find him thirty minutes later, curled up in the reading corner with *The Mystery of the Bloody Shoe*, or *The Case of the Empty Coffin*, or *The Detective's Diary*.

Somewhere in the middle of third grade, Ted had gotten hooked on mysteries. After he'd read all the ones at the school, he moved on to the mysteries in the children's collection at the town library. And after he'd read all *those*, he asked Mrs. Coughlin, the librarian, for more.

So she taught Ted how to connect with the interlibrary loan programs over the Internet. Suddenly Ted's library was a hundred times bigger than the one on Main Street. And that's why a fresh batch of books arrived every ten days. Mrs. Coughlin kept them behind her desk on a shelf marked, "Reserved for Ted Hammond."

He read two or three mysteries a week, but he didn't just read them. He solved them—or at least he tried.

Ted had developed his own mystery-solving system. When he got to the page at the exact middle of a mystery book, he stopped reading and picked up his pencil. First, he wrote down the names of all the characters. He carefully listed all the facts he knew so far. Then he tried to think of every possible way the case might end up. Finally, after he'd solved the mystery in his own mind, Ted zoomed through the second half of the book to see how the author solved it. And eight times out of ten, Ted got it right. Not bad for a twelve-year-old detective.

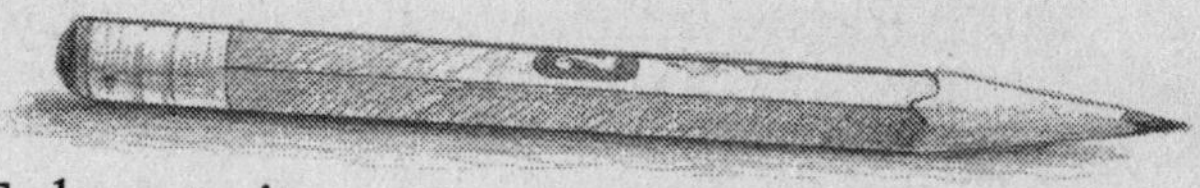

But in the spring of his sixth-grade year, the mysteries of real life were starting to demand Ted's attention. For example, just a few days ago at the dinner table, his dad had said, "How the heck am I supposed to keep this farm if the price of beef keeps droppin', and the price of fuel keeps goin' up? It's a mystery to me."

Then there was the mystery of how Red Prairie Learning Center was going to stay open next year after all the eighth graders left. That was a *big* mystery, and everyone in town wanted to solve it because, really, it was a matter of life and death. Out on the Great Plains in western Nebraska, people understand that if the school dies, the town dies too.

Back in April, Ted had heard talk at Clara's Diner one morning about a young family that wanted to buy a house on Hutchins Street, the old Chalmers place. The rumor was that they had four kids, ranging from second grade up to seventh. A week later word filtered back that they'd moved to Wheaton instead, thirty-eight miles west. So the survival of the school continued to be a matter of great suspense.

But on this particular Tuesday morning in May, the mystery that had Ted's full attention was that face. The one he'd seen at the Andersons' house.

By morning recess, Ted had worked out three possible explanations for that face in the window. By lunchtime, his list had grown to seven different solutions, but by two thirty he had crossed out three, including the idea that he might have seen a ghost. Ted was a practical, no-nonsense detective, and he certainly didn't believe in ghosts. That was a real girl he'd seen, so there had to be a real explanation.

As the school day ended, Ted thought about telling Mrs. Mitchell. Then he thought about riding his bike over to the town hall and telling Deputy Sheriff Linwood. And maybe that would have been the smartest and the safest thing to do.

But Ted had read a lot of mysteries. The police? And bossy grown-ups? They always seemed to get in the way of good detective work. No way was Ted going to let a bunch of other people spoil his investigation. But he wasn't going to be stupid about it either. If the situation looked like it might be dangerous, even a little bit, then he'd tell everyone else right away.

But for now, this was *his* mystery, and Ted wanted to solve it on his own.

Chapter 3

STAKEOUT

There's no such thing as a shortcut in Plattsford, Nebraska.

The streets and roads run straight north and south, or straight east and west. As the crow flies, the Anderson farm was only a mile and a half from his school. As the bike rolls, it was twice that far.

To get where he was going, Ted had to ride west on F Street for half a mile, then turn right and travel the full one-mile length of Main Street, then turn left onto County Road 7 and head out of town toward the intersection with Route 92.

But Ted didn't mind the distance. It was still a beautiful day, and out on the prairie, three miles isn't much. Besides, the ride gave Ted some time to come up with a plan.

Because there's also no such thing as sneaking up on someone in west central Nebraska. Most of the land is flat as a boot print. There are some little hills, but nothing that'll hide a kid on a bike for more than a minute or two. There are small stands of trees here and there, but mostly along creek beds, or where farmers have planted windbreaks. So Ted had to work out a way to get near the Andersons' house without being seen. Until he could prove otherwise, Ted was going to act as if someone was there. Watching.

He rode along the county road, and when he could see the roof of the farmhouse, he stopped and hid his bike in some weeds. Ted walked out into the tall grass until the Andersons' old barn stood directly between him and the farmhouse. Then, as he walked in a straight line toward the house, the barn kept him hidden from view. In case there was someone in the house. Watching.

The approach took about three minutes, including the time Ted spent flat on his stomach in the grass so people passing in a pickup couldn't see him. Because if someone saw him, chances were good they'd know him, and when he delivered tomorrow's paper at the diner, someone would almost certainly say, "Heard you were poking around at the Andersons' old place." The last thing a detective wants is publicity.

When Ted reached the north end of the barn, first he tugged the handle of the big sliding door, but it was chained shut from the inside. So he looked around until he found what he needed—a couple of wide boards that were weathered and shrunk up enough so he could get his fingers into the crack between them. The nails gave way as he pulled on the old siding, and he was able to pry one board out just far enough to wiggle through.

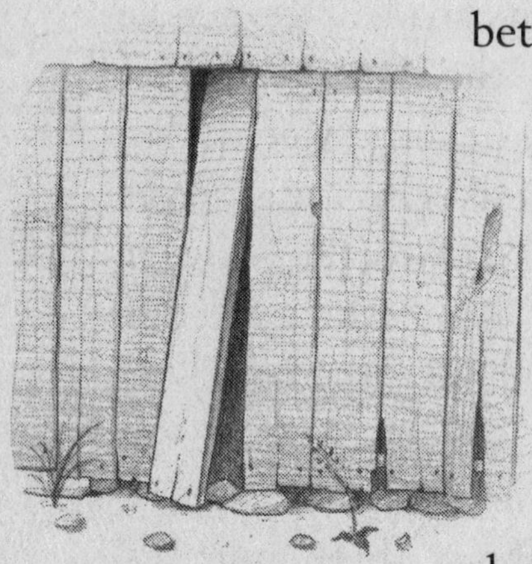

Ted had been in the Andersons' barn once before. He'd come with his dad to the auction. The bank had held the big sale on a Saturday, two days before the Andersons went to stay with relatives in Illinois. All the tools and farm equipment had been spread out on the front yard and the driveways and the paddock by the barn. There was furniture, too, loads of it, and an old upright piano.

Mr. Anderson had put on a brave face, and he even came over to Ted's dad to talk and joke a little, just like always. But he didn't fool Ted. The man was hurting inside, all torn up about having to leave his home and his land. And Mrs. Anderson had kept her eyes down and her lips pressed tightly together as she carried out box after box of the canning supplies and utensils and all the kitchen goods she wasn't going to need anymore.

Mandy Anderson was in fourth grade back then, and when Ted had smiled and said hi to her that day, she'd made a face at him and run back into the house.

It was over two years ago now, but Ted remembered it all so clearly. And he also remembered the promise he'd made himself as the auctioneer banged the gavel down again and again on that bright October morning: "This is never gonna happen at our farm—not at *my* farm."

Ted walked to the south end of the barn. He needed to get a good look at the house, but the wide double doors at this end were also chained, no spaces or cracks anywhere. To the left of the doors there was one window in a small storage room, but it was covered with plywood from the outside. Ted stepped back about ten paces, and, looking up, he saw a wide gap between the hayloft doors on the second story. Some ladder rungs had been nailed to a post, and thirty seconds later, he was up in the loft with one eye at the opening, scanning for signs of life.

His perch gave him a clear view of the backyard, the kitchen door, and the whole north end of the house. Ted wished he had his mom's little binoculars, the ones she used for bird-watching. With those he'd have been able to study the yard around the back porch for footprints. He saw some long grass that might have been stepped on recently, but that could have been deer. Or even rabbits. And the porch door looked like it was still boarded up tight, and so did all the ground floor windows he could see.

Nothing seemed disturbed or out of place, nothing obvious. No hint of recent human visitors.

But Ted wasn't in a hurry. Good detective

work takes patience. He had to be home by four to start his afternoon chores, but that gave him almost thirty minutes before he had to leave. So he dragged half a bale of hay into the right spot and tried to make himself comfortable. After another careful look at the house, Ted pulled a small black notebook from his back pocket, found a stubby pencil, looked at his watch, and made an entry.

May 18

3:19 p.m. Got a stakeout spot in the loft. Good view of the house. No activity.

Ten minutes crept by. Then Ted thought he heard a thump from the direction of the house. But it could have been from down below in the barn, too. Probably just that loose board banging in the afternoon breeze.

After five more minutes, Ted was tempted to go outside and sneak right up to the house. He wanted to do a walk-around, look at every window, check the area for footprints, put his ear against a wall and listen for sounds, things like that. Detective work. But he stayed put, and a while later he made another log entry.

3:41 p.m. No suspects observed.
One possible noise. No solid clues.

And as Ted tucked the notebook in his pocket he admitted that whoever he'd seen this morning might be long gone. And then he faced the fact that he might never know who it was. He even reconsidered the idea that he might have imagined that face.

He stood up and stretched, walked to the edge of the hayloft, and then carefully backed down the ladder to the ground floor of the barn. Time to head for home. Three new calves had been born in the last week, and two of them weren't steady enough to be out in the pastures yet. They were inside in two different holding stalls, one cow and her calf in each. The mothers took care of feeding the calves, but it was Ted's job to feed and water the cows and clean out the stalls every afternoon.

It was his favorite chore. The calves were shy and awkward, and they always made him laugh. And the animals liked him. His dad knew that, which is why he gave the job to Ted. The boy had a natural talent for putting animals at ease. Ted felt like he could tell what they were thinking. Sort of the way a good detective can figure out what's running through a criminal's mind. Except a newborn calf is probably less complicated than your average crook.

Back at the north end of the Andersons' barn, Ted found a short piece of iron pipe, and before he went outside, he used it on the loose board, bending the rusty nails down flat. He didn't want to get poked or scraped as he wriggled back through the opening. It would also make it easier to get in the next time.

Maybe he'd come back on Saturday. He'd bring some food and a thermos, and those binoculars. Then he could set up a real stake-out, take a good long look around, and figure out if anything was going on.

Ted pushed the board aside, and as he backed out, the sudden brightness of the afternoon sky almost blinded him. But he could see clearly enough to be sure it was a girl. She was right there, leaning with her back against the barn, waiting for him.

She wasn't big, and she wasn't holding a gun or a knife or an ax, but that didn't stop Ted's heart from pounding away like mad. As he blinked and tried to look brave, the girl glared at Ted the way a cat looks at a dog who's come one step too close.

And in a voice that sounded all twangy and nasal, she said, "Are you gonna tell on us?"

When Ted gulped and sort of stuttered, she stepped away from the barn and squared her shoulders at him, her fists tight, eyes narrow. "Well, *are* you? Are you gonna tell?"

And because he couldn't think, and because this girl looked like she might take a swing at him, Ted said the only thing that made sense at the moment. "T . . . tell? No . . . no, I'm not telling."

"Promise?"

Ted nodded. "Promise."

With his chest thumping and his mouth dry as straw, Ted was certainly surprised. And he was also confused by this sudden face-off with an angry girl.

Still, as a detective, Ted was thrilled. The Case of the Face in the Window had just blown wide open.

Chapter 4

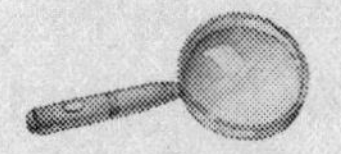

DETAILS

"Could prob'ly use some food—since you've got to come by here tomorrow anyway."

It was the last thing the girl said to him before he left, more like an order than a request.

And Ted nodded and said, "Sure thing."

He didn't like having to take off from the Andersons' farm in such a hurry. Especially since it might look like he was afraid. He didn't want that girl to think he was afraid. Because it wasn't true. No way.

But Ted had no choice about leaving. Chores are serious business on a working farm. He *had* to be home for chores at four o'clock, so he *had* to go.

The worst part was that he hadn't had time to get her whole story. Because that's what he wanted. He wanted the details, all of them. And he hadn't even gotten the girl's name. Or where she'd come from. Or how she'd ended up here in Plattsford.

Ted was out of breath from running back to where he'd stashed his bike, and when he hopped on and took off, the schoolbooks in his canvas newspaper bag banged against his legs as he pedaled for home. Even though it was partly a downhill ride, he knew he had to pump like mad if he was going to be on time.

Dozens of questions bounced around in his head, but Ted silenced all the noise except the wind in his ears and began reviewing the facts. Because a good detective always starts with the facts. And he knew that if he got his thoughts in order now, while everything was still fresh in his mind, it would be easier to write up his case notes later.

So Ted began at the beginning and talked himself through it.

When I came out of the barn, she was there, waiting. So . . . she must have seen me coming. Or been expecting me. Or heard me. Or all three.

And then she said, "Are you gonna tell on us?" She didn't say "tell on me." She said "on us." So there's her and someone else. At least one other person. Maybe more.

Ted had to swerve his bike to keep from running over a dead rabbit lying on the road. It hadn't been there on his way out. He hated to see any animal get hurt, but he understood it happened. He also understood that death was a regular part of life on a farm, especially if you raised cattle.

Still, just half an hour ago that rabbit had been skittering across a field, its feet barely touching the ground. And now it was crow food, pasted down flat on the highway. It made Ted think, and a quarter of a mile whizzed by before he got back to his detective work.

Okay . . . when the girl asked me the second time if I was going to tell? She had her fists up, and she looked like she was ready for a fight. So she's kind of tough. Maybe she's a boxer. Or a karate expert or something. Could be dangerous.

And the way she talked? She said, "Come on around the barn," and the word "around" sounded like "a-RAY-ound." And "barn" sounded like "BAW-ern." So she's from somewhere south. Maybe Texas or Louisiana. Or even Mississippi. Somewhere south.

And she asked if I could bring some food tomorrow. So whoever's there, either they don't have any money for food, or else they don't want to go into town. Or both.

As he rumbled over the railroad crossing at County Road and Main Street, Ted remembered the mystery he'd read about a boy who wanted to be a police sketch artist. The kid in the story had learned to look at someone for ten seconds, and then draw a perfect picture of them. He was like a human digital camera. That book had taught Ted a lot about noticing important details.

Ted had been with the girl for only a minute or two before he'd had to leave. And she'd taken charge and done most of the talking, asking him where he lived, and how far was it to town, and did he ride past here every day. But during the time she was quizzing him, Ted was busy taking mental notes. And now he played them back. He pretended he was talking to that kid, the one who could draw like a genius.

She's a white female, age . . . eleven to thirteen. Sort of a skinny build, a little more than five feet tall, same as me. Narrow face, pale skin with freckles on her upper cheeks, a thin nose that's sort of long, brown eyes, straight brown hair that comes down to her chin—sort of a grown-up haircut. And her teeth haven't had braces. Last seen wearing dirty pink running shoes, blue jeans with a little rip on the right knee, and a pale blue T-shirt with a yellow smiley face on it, except the smiley face is frowning. She chews her fingernails, and on her left—no, on her right hand there's a little silver ring with a small red stone in it.

Ted was pleased with himself for giving that fine description, and as he leaned his bike low and took the left turn onto Toronto Road a little too fast, he glanced at his watch—3:56. His dad's farm was exactly 1.1 miles up ahead, and the macadam road was flat and smooth.

Ted knew from years of experience that he was going to make it home on time. Because if you go fifteen miles an hour—which isn't that hard with a good bicycle on level ground—you travel one mile every four minutes.

At exactly four o'clock Ted's tires crunched on the gravel driveway of Hammond Acres, and Shep ran out to meet him, barking and running half circles the way a Border collie does. The driveway was neat, edged perfectly, and completely weed free—another one of Ted's chores.

As he put his bike away in the garden shed, Ted was still going over what he'd learned, reviewing every scrap of information to see if he'd missed anything. And he remembered something. Something he'd seen but hadn't really noticed, not until just now. It was there on the girl's left sneaker. Some writing.

Ted pushed himself, trying to sharpen the image, trying to make his fellow detectives proud of his excellent observation skills and his fantastic memory.

And as he walked across the yard toward the barn, the picture snapped clear. It was a name, written down near the sole of her shoe in faded black marker.

Suddenly the girl who was hiding out at the Anderson place was a little less mysterious.

Because now she had a name, and Ted knew what it was. And he also knew the first letter of her last name: *T*. So he had two pieces of real information.

Inside the barn now, he pulled off his school shoes and stepped into his work boots, and the cows and calves swung their heads and looked at him between the boards of the stall doors. Ted spoke, but he wasn't talking to the animals. He nodded politely and said, "Pleased to meet you, *Alexa*."

Chapter 5

BOY SCOUT BURGLAR

The rest of Ted's Tuesday went quickly. After his chores came dinner, then homework.

When his school assignments were finished, he could have watched a little TV, but instead Ted went right to his room and started a new case file about the girl, writing down every fact and observation and guess he could think of. New ideas rushed into his mind, and he kept asking himself, *Have I missed anything?* When he was sure he'd done a thorough job, Ted lay on his bed and opened his newest mystery book, *The Footprint on the Wall*. He let the book pull him into the action, glad to forget about that girl for a while.

After an hour Ted made himself stop. He wanted to keep reading, but there was one more thing he had to do before bed. It was time for a late-night raid.

Ted had been a Boy Scout for more than half

of his fifth-grade year, until the scoutmaster and his three sons moved from Hulton to Denver. But Ted still took his Scout Law seriously. A Scout is trustworthy. So that meant he had to be honest. But a Scout is kind, too. That meant he had to help that girl. And whoever else was out there with her.

So Ted, the kind and honest Scout, found an envelope in his room and wrote on it, "Homeless Food Fund." Then he put six dollars of his own money into the envelope, because he was going to pay back his mom for every bit of food he took.

With his conscience taken care of, Ted the Boy Scout was free to transform himself into Ted the cat burglar.

He had to get from his upstairs bedroom to the kitchen without being seen or heard by his brother Lucas, his sister Sharon, his dad, or his mom. And then he had to get back again with the food. He wished his newspaper shoulder bag was black instead of a weathered gray color. Cat burglars always prefer black.

What Ted lacked in equipment, he hoped to make up for with his skills. He floated along the upstairs hall, crept down the staircase, drifted through the parlor, and melted into the darkened kitchen. Then he slipped into the large pantry and pulled the door shut behind him without a sound.

Using the flashlight he had tucked into his belt, Ted scanned the shelves. He needed to build a balanced diet for at least two people. And he was guessing that they didn't have a stove, plates, bowls, or utensils.

So first he chose three cans of beef stew, because you could eat it cold, right from the can. With your fingers. He'd done that himself a few times on his first and only Boy Scout camping trip. Cold beef stew wasn't half bad.

A jar of applesauce would be good. Because if you tipped the jar and gave it a tap, you could sort of drink it. Drinkable fruit. Ted had done that a few times too.

The bread was on the top shelf, but he couldn't take a whole loaf. His mom would notice. So Ted peeled off six slices and tucked them into a plastic food bag.

There was a huge four-pound jar of Jif on the shelf, and Ted thought about loading a bunch of it into a plastic bag. Because that would be a great way to carry peanut butter. When you wanted some, all you'd have to do was poke a hole in a corner of the bag and squeeze. He could also dump some lumps of grape jelly into the bag. Very nutritious. And practical. You could take a bite of bread, then squirt in some PB&J, and mix it all right in your mouth. Bite, squeeze, chew, and swallow. Pretty cool.

But then Ted imagined the face of that girl as he handed her a plastic sack full of brown and purple goop. He decided to take some cheddar cheese instead.

Then the burglar remembered: *I keep calling her "that girl." Her name is Alexa.*

Chapter 6

CONVERSATION

On Wednesday morning Ted left home right at seven o'clock, a little earlier than usual. He wanted to be sure his mom didn't see his lumpy newspaper bag. As he rode away, the cans and the other food made it wobble around on his back.

There was a heavy ground fog, so Ted was extra careful about the trucks and cars he heard coming now and then. He had two of those bright, flashing LED bike lights, front and rear, and both were turned on. Still, with fog like this, the drivers couldn't see him until they were close.

But the fog was also good. It gave him a little cover for his secret mission.

When he was halfway up the hill on the county road, Ted slowed down. A truck was coming from behind, and he let it get well past before he stopped next to the battered mailbox with the name ANDERSON written in faded red letters.

The drive was overgrown with weeds and long grass, so Ted stayed on the hard-packed tread where he and his bike would leave less of a trail. Once he was well away from the road, he laid his bike down and walked to the back door.

The whole door frame was covered with a big sheet of plywood, screwed down tight. It seemed silly to knock on a door no one could open, but Ted did it anyway. *Tap, tap, tap.*

Ten seconds, then fifteen. Nothing.

He knocked again, louder, and then put his face near the plywood and called out, "Hey—anybody there? It's me, from yesterday."

And someone on the other side hissed, "Shhh! Go to the cellar door. And be quiet!"

It was the girl. Alexa. Definitely a Southern voice.

About ten feet to the left of the back porch there was a slanted stone and concrete bulkhead with steps that went down into the cellar. The bulkhead was covered with doors that opened upward. A length of chain with a rusty lock was looped through the wooden handles, but Ted looked closely and saw that the left handle had been pulled loose. The doors looked locked together, but they weren't.

He grabbed the handle on the right and when he lifted, there was the girl, looking up at him from the doorway at the bottom of the stone steps. Ted walked down until he was standing level with her.

She whispered, "You can't come in. My mom's still sleeping. And so's my little brother. I thought you'd be here early, so I slep' in the kitchen."

Ted took note—three people, a mom and two kids. And the girl was the older one. Alexa.

He tried a smile and said, "I didn't get your name yesterday. My name's Ted, Ted Hammond."

She smiled back, but it was faint and wary. "I'm . . . April. Pleased to meet you."

Ted thought, *Wrong name. Why's she lying?*

Going for the bold detective approach, Ted said, "Your name's not . . . Alexa?"

In a blink, the girl grabbed Ted by the front of his shirt and pushed him against the stone wall, her eyes wide with fear. Looking up toward the yard, and then straight into his eyes, she said, "Somebody follow you here? Who put y'up to this? You hear that name on the news or somethin'? Tell me!"

Ted pushed back until he wasn't against the wall, just to let her know he could. "It's right there on your shoe—Alexa T. I saw it yesterday. That's all. So hands off."

Embarrassed, but not apologetic, the girl dropped her hands. "Oh. Right."

The girl seemed a little flustered, and Ted thought it would be a good moment to get more information. He said, "So if your name's April, who's Alexa?"

"That's my mama, Alexa Thayer. These're her old shoes."

"And your little brother's here? How old's he?"

"He's ten. Artie."

Another mental note: Alexa, April, Artie. Somebody liked the letter *A*.

Ted said, "Did you tell your mom I was here yesterday?"

April shook her head. "She's too scared. If she knew someone'd come, we'd have left by now. But our food's about gone. So I took a chance."

Ted started pulling the supplies out of his shoulder bag, and she held the food in her arms. She was still wearing the same blue T-shirt with the frowning smiley face. He said, "It's not much."

"No," she said, "this is great. Thanks. 'Cept I'm not sure we can get these cans open. But there might be an opener, maybe on the wall somewhere in the kitchen. I'll figure it out."

Ted gave himself some detective demerits for not thinking of a can opener.

"Anything special you need?" he asked. "You warm enough at night? It still gets pretty cold."

"We've got sleepin' bags. We're okay. Just need food, mostly. And maybe some Sterno, those little cans for heatin' things up? My mom misses her coffee. And a gallon jug of water. But I don't want to be a bother." Then the girl's face reddened. "Some bathroom tissue would be good."

Ted nodded and looked away. "No problem. And it's not a bother. I come right by here. And I won't tell anybody. Like I promised."

Ted had another dozen questions he wanted to ask, but it wasn't the right time.

"Well, I've got to go get my newspapers. But I'll come back tomorrow—maybe this afternoon if I can." He held out his hand.

She hesitated but then shook it, and almost dropped a can of stew. Ted said, "Good to meet you, April."

"You too. Ted, right?"

He nodded. "Ted Hammond. See ya later."

He walked to his bike, and he heard the bulkhead doors close behind him, heard the chain rattle as the girl put the loose handle back in place.

As Ted got to the road and started pedaling, he tried to imagine April picking her way through the dark basement with the food in her arms. He imagined her finding the stairs and then going up into the Andersons' kitchen.

And he wondered if much daylight got in through the boarded-up windows. And he wondered where the mom and the little brother were sleeping. And then he wondered what the three of them were going to do in that empty house all day long.

Because Ted knew exactly what he was going to do today. He was going to go deliver his papers. And then he was going to school.

Chapter 7

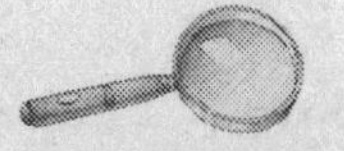

SIXTH-GRADE ISLAND

Mrs. Mitchell looked up from her social studies book. She was in a corner of the room talking about the end of the Civil War with the eighth graders. In the opposite corner of the room, the fourth graders were arguing. It looked like things had reached the boiling point.

"Carla, please read the fourth question out loud and then lead the discussion. I'll be right back."

Walking toward the fourth-grade corner, Mrs. Mitchell knew what the problem was. She always knew what the problem was with her fourth graders.

"Kevin, didn't I ask you all to read silently?" She stood over him with her hands on her hips.

Kevin said, "Shh—we're right in the middle of the best part. It's better this way. Hannah's gonna act out the part where the kid climbs out of the volcano."

Hannah lifted her nose and said, "I am *not* going to do that. I was *never* going to do that. It's *stupid*."

Mrs. Mitchell said, "That's enough, Hannah. Kevin, when I ask everyone to read silently, that's what has to happen. All right?"

Kevin shook his head. "No—really, because Hannah's got to act out that part, so she can fall, and then I get to come and rescue her. It's all worked out. We've only got six minutes before recess, and if everybody just keeps doing what I said, we can finish the story. It's almost over. Really. It's almost over. I know we can finish. Because it's all worked out. We're doing it as a play. Everything's perfect. Except we don't have costumes or anything. But that's okay. We're just imagining. And it's almost over."

Hannah, Lizzie, and Keith stood where Kevin had placed them on the reading rug. They knew Mrs. Mitchell was going to win this little battle, but they also knew they'd better wait until Kevin gave them permission to leave.

"Kevin?" Mrs. Mitchell kept her voice even. "Kevin, close your book and look at me. Look right in my face. Right here, in my eyes. Good.

Now, Kevin, I want you to just *read* the rest of the story, all right? Silently."

"But it's all worked out, really, and, and there's only four more pages. Or . . . or maybe six. But it's going fast. Hannah, come on. Don't you want to be in the play with me?"

Hannah shook her head. She didn't even want to be in the same universe with Kevin.

Mrs. Mitchell said, "Kevin? Look at my face. At my face, Kevin. Good. You have to sit down and read. Read the rest of the story. I need everyone to be quiet and read while I finish with the eighth graders. All right?"

Kevin rubbed a knuckle under his nose and then onto his pants. "All right. But it's not going to be any fun. It's just going to be like . . . like, words."

Mrs. Mitchell said, "It's going to be just fine, because you really are an excellent reader."

"Okay," said Kevin, rolling his eyes. "Everybody can sit back down at your own grubby little desks. Because we're going to *read* the end of the story now. We're going to read, read, read, and read until it's all over. Reading, reading, and more reading."

After Mrs. Mitchell was sure that Kevin was

actually going to sit and read for a few minutes, she went back to the other corner, where the eighth graders were now discussing something other than the Civil War.

Sitting near the middle of the large room, Ted had enjoyed watching that drama. He kept looking at Kevin, then he turned to watch Mrs. Mitchell take charge of the big kids again. And then he went back to his social studies assignment.

Ted had claimed the middle area of their large classroom. There were plenty of extra desks around, so Ted had pushed five of them together into a pentagon, with just enough room for one chair in the middle—an old swivel chair that he had found at a teacher's desk during a raid in one of the unused classrooms. Ted had a math desk, a science desk, a social studies desk, a reading desk, and a writing desk. Almost eight feet across, it was his command center, a small sixth-grade island.

Having five desks gave him plenty of storage space. There was room for his mystery books, his small collection of detective equipment, his newspaper bag, his lunch, and a supply of tools Ted kept in his science desk for emergency

bicycle repairs. Plus enough room for anything else he might need to have close at hand. Like schoolbooks.

Room one was sort of like a big aquarium, and Ted never got tired of watching the other fish. With five desks, he could face any direction he wanted to, depending on where the action was.

His central location also gave Ted lots of practice at observing people. Reading all the Sherlock Holmes mysteries had taught him that good detective work is mostly watching and listening, and learning to notice important details. And writing things down.

In room one Ted had learned how to watch people so they didn't know he was paying attention, an art that detectives always find useful. And sometimes he sat near Carla and

Joan and practiced his secret listening skills. He was amazed by some of the things eighth-grade girls talked about. And in a top secret red notebook in his writing desk, Ted kept a file about every person in room one. Even Mrs. Mitchell.

From things his teacher had said in class, and from careful observation, Ted knew that Mrs. Mitchell's husband's name was Robert, and that he worked for the Bureau of Land Management, and that she thought his job made him spend too much time away from home. Mrs. Mitchell's mom and dad lived in Lincoln now, but she had grown up on a wheat farm in Cherry County, and she had graduated from Chadron State College. Ted knew Mrs. Mitchell had two children, a boy who was a freshman at Wayne State and a girl who was a sophomore at the same regional high school his own brother and sister attended. His teacher was forty-six years old, her birthday was April 12, and she had been teaching school for eighteen years—the last eight years at Red Prairie. Mrs. Mitchell was five feet six inches tall, with brown hair, dark brown eyes, and a nose with a bump on it; and she had a tiny white scar on her forehead, just above her left eyebrow. She drove a dark blue Chevy Cavalier, license plate number PL 7865. Her first name was Barbara. And she wore size eight shoes.

Ted finished his social studies, and with five minutes before recess, he chewed on the end of his pencil and aimed his mind at his real-life mystery, the one out on County Road 7.

Because something April had said had been bothering him all morning. When he'd asked her if her name was Alexa, she got mad and asked him if he had heard that name on the news.

Her mom's name. On the news.

A person whose name is on the news could be in trouble, like maybe lost or in an accident. But there's another kind of trouble that gets a name onto the news—trouble with the law. Because bank robbers get their names on the news. So do kidnappers and burglars. And murderers.

Ted wasn't sure he wanted to meet April's mom. Alexa. And it sounded like she didn't want to meet him, either. April had said she was scared, said she would have left the Andersons' if she'd known Ted had been there.

But Ted set his fears aside and began to think about the problem of getting more supplies for them. Because he'd told April he would.

He turned to his writing desk, pulled out a clean piece of paper, and started a shopping list. After school he could go to the E&A Market, load up, and then ride out there again.

April had asked for water. Had to have water.

And toilet paper. Also a must.

They'd need bread.

And more soup, the kind with plenty of meat and vegetables.

And a can opener.

Maybe a flashlight. Or some candles.

And instant coffee. And Sterno.

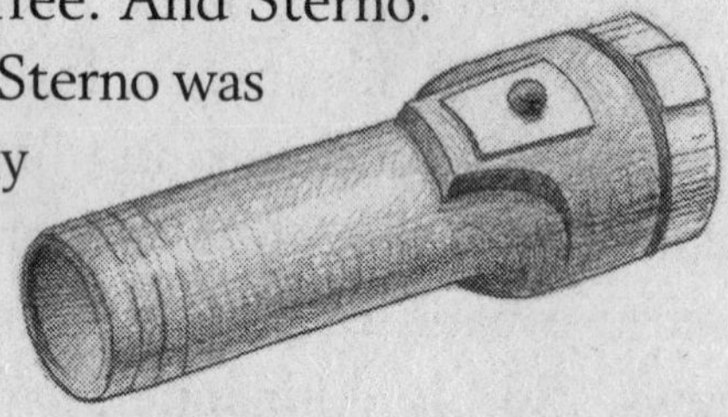

Ted knew what Sterno was because his family had gone to the Sunday buffet at the Holiday Inn over in Hulton once, and he had asked the chef about the little flaming cans under the serving trays.

His shopping list seemed to be getting longer and longer, and all of a sudden Ted understood why: *Three people multiplied by breakfast, lunch, and dinner—that's . . . nine meals a day! That's a TON!*

The size of what he'd volunteered to do hit Ted like a sack of grain. And all this was going to take money, too. Not to mention time.

But he'd said he'd help. He'd shaken hands with April and he'd said, "See ya later." So it wasn't like he had a choice.

Because a Scout is trustworthy.

And so is a detective. And a paperboy.

Chapter 8

BADGES

Ruby Cantrell tried to mind her own business. She really did. Customers at the E&A Market could buy anything they wanted to, as long as they had the money. And as long as those teenagers weren't trying to get ahold of things they shouldn't. Because the E&A Market was a genuine general store that sold everything from pantyhose to shotgun shells, from sugar cubes to antifreeze. Didn't matter to Ruby what anybody bought. If Mrs. Kellins wanted to buy six jars of face cream at a time, it wasn't anybody's business but her own. Probably made Mrs. Kellins feel good to see a whole year's supply of beauty products stacked up there in her bathroom. And if Mr. Arliss bought seven gallons of chocolate milk every single week, well, so what? The man liked chocolate milk. Ruby tried to pay it no mind. She was just the cashier.

But when young Teddy Hammond started unloading his shopping cart on Wednesday afternoon, Ruby felt like she had to butt in. "You know, honey, your mom never buys this kind of bathroom tissue. She gets the one with the bluebirds on it. You maybe want to take this back?"

Ted smiled and said, "No, it'll be okay."

Ruby shook her head, but she punched the price into the keypad, and the cash register went, *beep*.

Then she rang up six cans of soup, a hand-cranked can opener, oatmeal raisin granola bars, a gallon of spring water, a loaf of bread, four tins of evaporated milk, a jar of cheddar cheese spread, four apples, three cans of tuna fish, instant coffee, plastic spoons and knives, a stack of paper cups, six Snickers bars—it sure seemed like a strange shopping list.

Ruby stopped short and looked Ted in the face. "You're buyin' matches? And candles?"

Ted had an answer ready. "Yup, and the Sterno cans, too. I was a Boy Scout—you know, Be Prepared. That's what I always tell my mom. Gonna be some big storms this spring."

Beep . . . beep, beep.

Ted paid the bill, and he made a big show of folding the receipt and putting it in the envelope he'd taken the money from, just like his mom did when she shopped.

That made Ruby feel better.

Ted carried the two plastic bags out to his bike, pleased that he had earned his Shopping for Strangers merit badge with flying colors. Because that's how he was thinking about the afternoon's activities. It was like earning merit badges in Boy Scouts. If you met a certain set of requirements, then you earned a merit badge. In the short time he'd been part of a troop, Ted had earned badges in Crime Prevention, Animal Science, and Weather.

Next on his list for today, Ted was going for his Secret Transportation badge. He had to haul all this stuff out to the Anderson place without arousing suspicion.

The groceries made a heavy load, but Ted managed to fit everything into his big shoulder bag. Except the loaf of bread. He kept that in a plastic bag and hung it from his handlebars so it wouldn't get smooshed.

Ted was worried about making another trip along County Road 7. Someone was sure to notice and think it was odd, him going out that way twice in one day. But people were used to seeing the boy ride around town with his newspaper bag, so Ted earned his Secret Transportation badge without a hitch. And he made certain that no one saw him turn in at the old farm.

But when Ted laid his bike down behind the Andersons' house, he didn't hurry over to knock at the kitchen door. He took his time. Because the next merit badge felt a little scary.

Ted wasn't sure he wanted to meet April's mom.

Alexa. He was dying of curiosity, but Ted had read plenty of stories about people who needed to hide out. What if Alexa really was a criminal? What if she'd been holding up a bank somewhere . . . and she got hit by a bullet during the getaway . . . and now she had to lay low with her arm in a sling until things cooled off, before she could go find a doctor? What if April's mom was like Ma Barker from the 1920s, the boss of a whole gang of crooks? Or what if she was an old lady with a tattoo on her arm who'd just broken out of prison?

And what if someone had been making April tell lies about everything? Maybe there was a desperate band of international jewel thieves hiding out at the Anderson place after a big heist in Scotts Bluff or Omaha. And maybe April and her family had been in the wrong place at the wrong time, and they all got taken hostage. What about that? Because stuff like that happened all the time in mystery books.

Ted had reached the kitchen porch. He pushed all the fears out of his mind and pulled himself back to reality. Because whatever else was going on at this house, he'd made a promise. He had promised a girl that he'd bring her some food. And he was going to keep that promise.

No matter what, it was time to earn his Meet the Mom badge.

So Detective Ted Hammond knocked on the back door.

Chapter 9

ALEXA

April was wearing a different shirt now—blue and white, long sleeves, with a NASCAR picture on the front and "Texas Motor Speedway" written across the back. So it was a shirt and it was a clue, too. Ted also noticed that this shirt wasn't much cleaner than the one with the frowning smiley face had been. He remembered how dirty his own clothes had been when he'd come back after a week at the 4-H camp. It's hard to stay clean when you're away from home.

Ted followed April through the cellar and up the stairs. The kitchen was empty except for a wooden packing crate in one corner with a red backpack sitting on top of it. On the floor beside the crate was a sleeping bag folded in half with the corner of a pink pillowcase poking out the top. Ted realized he was looking at April's bedroom.

The place didn't smell very good. Not horrible, just not fresh. It looked like someone had tried to clean the area a little. But you need a broom and a mop and clean water to spruce up a kitchen.

And windows that'll open to let in some air.

April pointed to the kitchen counter. "You can put your bag there. Come on into the front room."

Ted was surprised to see there was some furniture in the living room. There was a gray and white mattress on the floor over by the staircase, and someone had left a rolled-up sleeping bag on it. In the far corner there was a recliner chair with stuffing coming out where the vinyl was ripped. That looked like another sleeping area, probably the little brother's.

In the corner to his right Ted saw a jumble of things that the Andersons hadn't bothered to take with them. It was the sort of stuff that sits by the road after a garage sale with a sign that says FREE. A lamp with a torn shade. Two shopping bags full of baby clothes. A ripped black-and-red checkerboard. Three or four battered aluminum pots and pans. Some paperback books that had gotten wet. A card table with one bent leg.

Ted also saw the things April's family had brought with them: two small plastic suitcases, one pink, one bright blue, and a large dark green duffel bag. It wasn't much.

"Mama, this is Ted."

Alexa walked over and took Ted's hand. "Well, I am pleased to make your acquaintance. April tells me you're a very nice young man. We sure appreciate what you brought to us. Real kind of you. And April said you promised you wouldn't tell anybody we're here, is that right?"

Ted nodded. "Yes, ma'am. Pleased to meet you, too." Her hand felt cold.

April's mom didn't look like any criminal Ted had ever read about. Or seen on TV. She seemed tiny, hardly an inch taller than he was. She had pale yellow hair, too yellow to be real, and when Ted looked in her face, he mostly saw her eyes, brown and big.

But Ted could see what April had meant about her mom being scared. Her eyes were sort of shaky, and the smile didn't seem natural.

Even so, it was a friendly smile, and her teeth were bright white, almost like they'd been painted. She had on jeans and a baggy, pale green sweater pulled up to her elbows. Her hands were long and thin, and the pink fingernail polish was mostly worn off.

She wasn't much like the moms Ted knew around town, and she wasn't scary at all. It was hard to imagine her breaking the law. Still, every detective knows you can't go just by the way things look.

Alexa waved her hand at the room around them. "Sorry I can't offer you a cold drink and make you feel at home, but we're kind of roughin' it." After an awkward pause, she said, "This is Artie. Artie, say hi to Ted."

April's little brother was lying on his sleeping bag near a patch of light coming through a broken board on one of the front windows. He kept reading his X-Men comic book. He was thin, same as April, except he had blond hair instead of brown, wearing jeans and a red T-shirt, no socks, no shoes.

In a sharper tone, Alexa said, "Artie, I *said* say hi to Ted here." Artie waited another three seconds. Then he looked up, put a fake-looking smile on his face, said, “Hi,” and went right back to his reading. Artie wasn’t about to pretend that he was having a good time.

Ted said, “Um . . . I brought some more food and things. Probably not near enough, but . . . well, I wasn’t sure how long you’re going to be here.”

Ted hoped saying that would get her talking about her plans.

But Alexa just smiled and said, “Oh, I’m sure whatever you brought’ll be just fine. And that reminds me—here’s some money.” She dug into the front pocket of her jeans and pulled out a crumpled five-dollar bill.

Ted started to say no, but Alexa grabbed his hand and pushed the money into his palm. She said, “Now, I know this isn’t near enough, but we don’t want to be any more of a burden than we have to be.”

Ted said, “Thank you, ma’am,” and he decided then and there that Alexa hadn’t robbed any banks recently.

Alexa smiled again and said, “And I’m keepin’ count so I can pay you back just as soon as I get to an ATM. ’Cause we’ve got money, believe it or not.”

Everyone had run out of things to say.

So Ted said, "Well, I've got to get going. I've got chores. At home." And right away, he wished he hadn't said, "At home." It seemed unkind.

Alexa nodded. "Oh, I understand. I grew up on a ranch down near El Paso, and chores won't wait, will they? April'll walk you out. You two prob'ly have things you want to talk about, anyway."

Ted cringed when she said that, but he smiled and said, "Well, so long."

Turning away, Ted thought, *Why do moms always say that? What in the world would I have to say to some girl? Except that I do have a ton of questions for her.*

As a detective, Ted had plenty to talk about. And ask. Because so far, everybody was acting like he should just stop by with food now and then and pretend like it was the most natural thing in the world for a mom and two kids to be hanging out in an empty house.

In the kitchen, Ted began pulling the supplies out of his bag. That's when he noticed an old cast-iron pump on the drainboard at the sink. His kitchen had one of those too. He nodded at it

and said, “Y’know, that could fix your water problems here.”

April shook her head. “Almost wore out my hands on it. Just makes a hissing sound.”

A lot can break and wear out around a farm, and Ted had always watched and asked questions when his dad fixed things. He said, “Gasket’s probably dried out.”

He opened the gallon bottle of spring water, raised the curved pump handle, and then poured a cup or two into the hole where the round rod went into the top of the casing. “That’ll swell up the gasket. In about fifteen minutes, pour in another cup, and then pump it twenty or thirty times, real fast. Just might work. And if it doesn’t, I’ll bring some tools and put on a new gasket. Bucket of water’s all you need to make a bathroom work. That’s what we do if the power goes out. ’Cause if you have plenty of water, it’ll be a lot easier here.” Then he added, “In case you’re planning to stay a while.”

Ted let that thought hang in the air a few

seconds, then picked up his canvas bag and said, "Well, gotta go."

April followed him down the stairs and then through the basement and out into the backyard. As he picked up his bike, she said, "It's nice a' you not to ask a lot of questions."

She started to turn toward the house, then stopped.

April began talking, and it was like she wanted to get it all out in one breath. "My dad is a soldier, and he got killed in Iraq. That was about a month ago. Then this army friend of his tried to come and move in with us. 'Cause he thinks he loves my mom. We called the police, and he stopped bothering, but Mama was upset, and mostly just sad, and she decided we had to go to Colorado, to her sister's. That's why we left Texas. In the middle of the night. And the car started smokin' real bad back in Kansas, and then it just stopped. We got a ride from a lady in a big RV, but she had to turn north about three miles up the road. So we saw the sign, and we started walkin' toward town, and it was dark, and then we came here to ask for a phone 'cause my mom's cell phone's dead. Ended up comin' inside. And that's when my mom got scared and started thinking Lorne might be trackin' us. That's the guy's name, back in Texas. 'Cept he isn't trackin' us, 'cause Lorne couldn't track a cockroach in a bucket. But Mama decided to just stay put for a while anyway."

April shrugged. "And that's it. That's all there is." Then she added, "But my mom's not sick or anything. She's just scared, is all. And with Daddy gone, it's extra hard now. On everybody. You saw Artie. He's mad, and he's got a mean mouth on him too."

Ted didn't know what to say. It was a lot to deal with. All of a sudden he felt like he was in a movie about some homeless people. But it wasn't a movie. It was happening right in his own town. And he was in the middle of it.

He had to say something. "Well, I'm glad I can help out. And I'm glad it was me who saw you, instead of somebody else."

April nodded and said, "Me too." Then she smiled.

And Ted the detective made a mental note that April had just smiled her first real smile.

He climbed on his bike, and as he rode out

along the overgrown front drive, Ted was still thinking about that smile, and thinking about April's story, too.

Which were the wrong things to be thinking about at that moment. Ted should have been thinking about the car that was coming up the hill from town.

As he reached the old mailbox, the car was right there, and as Ted looked up, so did the driver. And then the driver smiled and waved at him.

The car was a dark blue Chevy Cavalier, license plate number PL 7865. And the driver was Ted's teacher, Mrs. Mitchell.

Chapter 10

PROSPECTS

The second Ted looked up and saw Mrs. Mitchell's face, he knew big trouble was headed his way. As her car sped away, his teacher was probably already calling Deputy Linwood on her cell phone. The police cruiser was going to show up any second, with blazing lights and both sirens wailing. He was going to be arrested for trespassing. And Alexa and her family? They'd be hauled off to the police station. For breaking and entering. And trespassing. The mom would go to jail, the kids would get sent to an orphanage. And April was going to think it was all his fault.

The truth of the situation was very different.

Mrs. Mitchell saw Ted, smiled, waved, and an instant later dropped him out of her thoughts. Completely.

Mrs. Mitchell had other things to think about. She was on her way to Wheaton. She had to try to convince the school superintendent not to close Red Prairie Learning Center. Because how would she and her husband pay for their son's college if she had to stop teaching? And if she lost her teaching job, what would happen to her pension? And her health care? And if she *kept* teaching, but had to drive the seventy-five-mile round-trip to a school in Wheaton, how was *that* going to change her family's budget?

Forty-five minutes later Mrs. Mitchell was sitting across a table from Mr. Seward, the superintendent of the district that included her one-room school. He didn't have good news.

"You know how it is, Barbara. It doesn't make sense to pay a teacher and keep a school open for five students. If you had nine kids again, we could make the numbers work—and twelve or fifteen students would be about perfect. I hate to make those Plattsford kids ride over here on a bus next year, but they'll fit right into classrooms we're already paying for. And every one of those students will bring the Wheaton schools fourteen thousand dollars of state aid."

Mrs. Mitchell flashed a bitter smile and said, "And don't forget all the money you're going to save when you don't have to pay my salary anymore."

Mr. Seward held up his hands. "Now, don't put it like that. This is just what happens when a town gets small, that's all."

Mrs. Mitchell kept pushing. "And what about the town? Do you think new families will ever settle in Plattsford again if they know their kids will have to ride a school bus for over two hours every day? Kindergartners and first graders riding all that way? The town's barely alive as it is. Close the school and it'll be like slamming the lid on a coffin." Mrs. Mitchell calmed herself and then said, "You know, we've got three four-year-olds in Plattsford, and at least that many three-year-olds. Just wait another year or two, and things will turn around. I know they will. Because if that school closes, I don't think it'll ever start up again."

Mr. Seward puffed up his cheeks and let out a slow breath. He shrugged and said, "You know I'm sorry. I'm not doing this on purpose. But let's not give up yet, all right? I promise we'll do everything we can to keep the school open. But I can't hold out a whole lot of hope, either. I'm just being honest."

The ride home seemed even longer to Mrs. Mitchell, and her thoughts were as gloomy as the low clouds gathering in the east.

It was beginning to get dark by the time she turned left off of Route 2 onto County Road 7. And when her headlights caught the reflector nailed to the post of the Andersons' mailbox, Mrs. Mitchell remembered. She'd seen Ted Hammond coming out of that driveway a few hours ago.

Teachers look into children's faces all day long. A teacher can spot a confused child from thirty feet away. A teacher can tell if a kid is angry or upset. A teacher can look at a face and know if a student is lying or telling the truth—sort of like a good detective.

And Mrs. Mitchell was an expert at reading faces—especially eyes.

So when she remembered seeing Ted, Mrs. Mitchell made herself a mental note, just like a detective would. She thought, *I'll have to ask Ted what he was doing out here. I don't want that boy getting into trouble.*

Because even though she had locked eyes with Ted for less than a second, Mrs. Mitchell knew what she had seen.

Ted Hammond had looked guilty.

Chapter 11

FAIR AND SQUARE

Room one seemed especially small to Ted on Thursday morning.

In a school with only nine students, there's no way for a kid to lay low. Ted couldn't make himself invisible, but his assignments provided pretty good camouflage. First he slogged away on his historical fiction book report at his social studies desk. Then he dug into his booklet of extra-credit word problems at his math desk. He kept his eyes only on his work, and he kept a serious look on his face.

Ted had been surprised the evening before. He'd felt sure that Deputy Linwood was going to track him down and give him a little ride in the police cruiser. Mrs. Mitchell had definitely seen him at the Anderson farm. She had looked right at him. She'd even waved. She must have known he shouldn't be there. Ted had gone to bed Wednesday night feeling certain that by morning he'd be in jail, right next to the cell holding April and her mom and brother.

But nothing had happened.

He was even more surprised at the start of the school day when Mrs. Mitchell didn't say anything to him, didn't even give him a funny look. It was like nothing had happened. But he kept clear of his teacher as much as possible anyway. He went about his business. When Mrs. Mitchell spoke to him, he spoke back. When she smiled at him, he smiled back. Everything seemed fine.

By lunchtime Ted was starting to feel like the danger had passed. He was practically home free, because after lunch on Thursday it was time for outdoor cleanup.

There hadn't been a custodian at Red Prairie Learning Center for three years. Before then, a janitor from the Wheaton schools had driven a truck over once a week, run a dust mop around the floor, washed the chalkboards, and then driven the thirty-seven miles back to Wheaton. It wasn't a good system, and the school never seemed well cared for.

Then Mrs. Mitchell had read an article about how teachers and children in Japanese villages take care of their own schools, inside and out. The article said it made the children feel more responsible, provided a good learning activity, and helped create school spirit.

Mrs. Mitchell liked the idea, so she had written a proposal. She and her students would do a little classroom cleaning every day, like dusting and washing desks and sweeping the floors. Then there would be an outdoor work period every Thursday afternoon, and a thorough indoor cleaning session every Friday afternoon. That way the yard and the classroom would be tidy and clean at the start of each new week. And for occasional jobs like mowing or snowplowing, the school district could hire the town hall handyman and pay him by the hour.

Mr. Seward had liked the idea too, mostly because it saved the district money. And once the plan was put into action, the Wheaton school board even increased Mrs. Mitchell's salary a little—something that hadn't happened for a long time.

Ted enjoyed the outdoor work more than the classroom chores. And on this particular Thursday, being outside felt great to him. If he could stay away from his teacher, maybe she'd forget all about yesterday afternoon. Ted had chosen a job he could do alone, far away from where Mrs. Mitchell was leading the fourth-grade leaf-raking brigade.

Ted carried the two heavy outside doormats over to the low chain-link fence and draped them over the top rail. Then he began hitting them with an old tennis racket, knocking out the dried mud and grass. It wasn't exactly fun, but today it felt like the best job in the world. It felt like he'd been given a free pass to an hour of complete safety.

That feeling didn't last.

He turned around, and there was Mrs. Mitchell.

She said, "Hi, Ted" and began raking up some dry leaves that had blown against the fence. But that wasn't why she had come to this part of the schoolyard.

She said, "I've been wanting to speak to you alone. Do you mind if I ask why you were coming out of the driveway at the Anderson farm yesterday afternoon?"

Ted gulped. He said, "Um . . ." and then took another three whacks at a doormat.

Ted had known Ruby Cantrell was going to ask him why he was buying matches and candles at the market, so he had planned out what to tell her in advance. Something that made sense. Something that wasn't a lie.

But this was different. He'd been thinking ever since yesterday about what to say to his teacher. He had nothing, and it was already taking him much too long to answer Mrs. Mitchell. Because it never takes long to tell the truth. No matter what he said now, it was going to sound like a lie.

Ted gulped again and said, "I was there . . . well, it's sort of a Boy Scout project I'm doing."

Ted felt like he had been using his Boy Scout connection a lot in the past few days. But Mrs. Mitchell didn't know that. And what he'd just told her was true . . . sort of.

Ted kept beating clouds of dust out of the doormats so he wouldn't have to look at his teacher.

"Hmm," she said. "I thought the Scout troop shut down when the Kyler boys moved away."

"Well, yeah," said Ted, "but I'm still a Scout. You know, on my own."

"Oh. That's interesting. And this project? What's it about?"

Ted gulped a third time.

If he told his teacher the truth, he'd have to break his promise to April. And her mom. And if he lied, it would have to be a whopping big one to get Mrs. Mitchell off the case.

Ted felt awful. He didn't want any lies at all, big or small.

Mrs. Mitchell could see Ted was upset. He had a two-handed grip on the tennis racket now, and he was giving the doormats a terrible thrashing.

Ted thought, *I can't lie to Mrs. Mitchell. But I promised I wouldn't tell. I promised. I have to keep my promise.*

And in the stress of the moment, with the dusty tennis racket in mid-swing, Ted saw what a powerful grip a promise can have.

And not just on him. A promise can grab hold of anyone.

Even a teacher.

He stopped beating the doormat, turned to Mrs. Mitchell, and looked her right in the eye.

He wanted her to see he was telling the truth. "Mrs. Mitchell, I can't tell what my project's about because I promised I'd keep it a secret. But I can make you a promise too. I promise that I'm not doing anything wrong out there. Not one thing." And then Ted raised his right hand with the first two fingers held up in a salute. "Scout's honor."

Mrs. Mitchell looked into Ted's face. She loved this boy. She loved all her students, even the eighth-grade boys and girls—who sometimes seemed to do their best to be unlovable. Didn't matter. She loved them all.

As far as she knew, Ted had never lied to her, not once in all the years she'd known him. And she had no reason to think he was lying now. He was the most dependable child in room one. His work was always done well, and done on time. He studied for tests, he did his outside reading. And he delivered the newspaper to her front porch every morning, without fail.

Still, something odd was going on. And it made her uneasy to accept this promise without knowing more.

Mrs. Mitchell asked, "Aren't there 'No Trespassing' signs all over that property?" Because then she could tell Ted to keep away from the place just as a matter of obeying the law. Because a Scout is obedient. Her son had been a Boy Scout too.

Ted shook his head. "Nope. Not one."

Mrs. Mitchell recalled reading about that in the *Weekly Observer*. The banks had so many abandoned properties on the Great Plains, they had stopped putting up NO TRESPASSING signs to help cut their costs.

She said, "Ted, I know you're a good boy, but I don't want you getting into trouble out there, that's all."

He said, "Oh, I'm not. Really."

Ted felt like he'd hooked a fish, but it wasn't in the canoe yet. Because if Mrs. Mitchell picked up the phone and asked Deputy Linwood to drive out to the Anderson place and take a look around, his so-called project would be finished.

And then Ted saw what to do.

He said, "Mrs. Mitchell, if you promise that you'll keep everything a secret, then I can tell you. About my project."

Now it was Mrs. Mitchell on the spot.

Looking into Ted's face, she saw how much

he trusted her. And she saw how important her answer would be. If she refused to make this promise, would Ted stop trusting her? And what if she did promise, and then what if Ted told her about something . . . bad? What then? Because it would be awful if she had to break a promise. But hadn't Ted already promised he wasn't doing anything wrong?

A person who teaches school for eighteen years becomes a good judge of character. So Mrs. Mitchell held out her hand.

She said, "You already promised you're not doing anything wrong, and as long as that's true, I promise I won't tell anyone about your project. That sound fair?"

Ted said, "Fair and square," and he shook Mrs. Mitchell's hand.

If Ted or Mrs. Mitchell could have guessed how complicated their new partnership would become, that handshake might have never happened.

But it did. Because a promise is a powerful thing.

Chapter 12

SLEEPLESS

It was almost midnight. Mrs. Mitchell heard her husband upstairs in bed, snoring away. But that wasn't why she couldn't sleep. Mrs. Mitchell couldn't sleep because about ten hours ago she had stood in the schoolyard and made a promise to a twelve-year-old boy.

And now she wished she hadn't.

She took a sip of hot chocolate and then said out loud, "*What* was I thinking?"

After they exchanged promises and shook on it, Ted Hammond had given his teacher a short explanation of his charity project. He'd told her about seeing the girl at the Anderson farmhouse, about going back and meeting her, about meeting the mom and the little brother, about learning that their dad had died in Iraq, about how they'd left Texas, and how there was this sort of boyfriend who might be trying to find them. And Ted had been helping this homeless family by taking them food and supplies.

Sounded simple enough.

But as Ted had told her this, warning bells had begun ringing in Mrs. Mitchell's head. Because she heard *this* story: A mom—who might be mentally unbalanced—was having trouble caring for two children, and all three of them were living in an abandoned house. Illegally. In filthy conditions. While a boyfriend hunted for them. And *he* might be mentally unbalanced too.

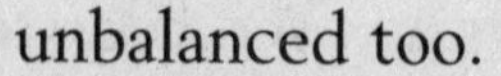

Sitting at her kitchen table, Mrs. Mitchell began imagining what the people at Nebraska Health and Human Services would say about this situation. And she felt pretty sure that they would listen to Ted's story and begin to use words like "neglect." Or "endangerment."

And now that Mrs. Mitchell knew Ted's story, she couldn't sit by and be a spectator. Because if anything happened to those people, especially to the children . . .

And that's when Mrs. Mitchell decided that she had to do something.

Right away.

Two miles away in a farmhouse out along Toronto Road, someone else was wide awake at midnight.

Because as Ted had told his teacher about April and her mom and brother, Mrs. Mitchell's mouth had kept smiling, and her head had kept on nodding. But her eyes? Her eyes had been cloudy.

And now Ted was trying to put himself into his teacher's mind, which wasn't easy to do. But he made himself think like a detective who had to solve a mystery. He thought about all the clues, and he reviewed everything he knew about Mrs. Mitchell.

And all at once Ted got a peek at how she was probably thinking: He felt pretty sure Mrs. Mitchell would be worried about those kids. Because that's what teachers do. Moms, too. And Mrs. Mitchell was both a teacher *and* a mom.

And then Ted realized that if Mrs. Mitchell was *really* worried about April and Artie, she'd feel like she had to do something. She'd tell somebody. Like the police. Or the welfare people. She'd tell them—promises or no promises.

He knew he had to do something.

But what?

Should he warn April? He could do that first thing in the morning.

Except, if he warned her, he'd have to tell how he broke his promise about not telling anybody.

And then Ted tried to decide which would be worse: seeing April's face when she knew he had broken his promise, or seeing April and her mom and little brother sitting in the backseat of a police car.

He made his decision. Then he turned over, and after another fifteen minutes of tossing and turning, the Boy Scout detective paperboy finally got to sleep.

Chapter 13

CRIME SCENE

Riding along County Road 7 early Friday morning, Ted was on his way to talk to April and Alexa and Artie. He had to tell them they had to leave. Today. Right away.

As the Andersons' barn came into view, Ted rehearsed his speech. *This is all my fault. I should have been more careful, because my teacher saw me when I left here Wednesday afternoon. And then she asked me why I was here, and I had to tell her what I was doing so she wouldn't call my mom and dad or anybody. And I made her promise to keep everything a secret, but I'm pretty sure she's gonna feel like she has to tell other people. Like the police. So you've got to pack up and get out. Maybe go and get a ride from someone out on Route 2. Or walk west about two miles to the truck stop so you can use the pay phone and call your relatives in Colorado. Because it's not safe to stay here anymore. And I'm sorry. I'm really sorry. I'm so sorry.*

When Ted swung his bike around the back corner of the farmhouse, he slammed on the brakes. He stood there and stared, trying to understand. Because both cellar doors were wide open, spread out like the wings of a giant moth.

Ted dropped his bike and dashed down the cellar steps, almost tripping over something in the darkness. And as he ran up the stairs toward the kitchen he yelled, "April? Artie? It's me, Ted. Alexa?"

But he already knew.

The kitchen was empty. No sleeping bag, no pink pillowcase.

Ted rushed to the front room. No plastic suitcases, no green duffel bag.

They were gone.

He tried to stop breathing so fast. He had to slow down. Ted made himself look around the room. He tried to think like a detective. Was there any sign of a struggle? That's a question they asked in mystery books. But this wasn't a book, and it was hard for Ted to tell anything. The room was messy, just like before. Except they were gone.

Ted made himself walk calmly back to the kitchen. He made himself turn his head and notice things. The can opener he had brought was lying on the counter. The gallon jug of water sat by the sink, empty. Ted tried the pump handle a few times, felt some resistance, and after six or eight strokes, water. So he'd been right about the gasket needing to swell up. Having gotten the pump to work wasn't much comfort. They were still gone.

Ted felt like he should open every drawer, look in every cabinet, try to figure out what had happened. But why bother?

Back outside, Ted looked around the yard. And that's when he saw the tracks.

A car had left tire tracks. Or maybe a pickup truck. Tire tracks, plain as day, because the ground was soft and the long grass was still bent over.

Ted stepped to one side and looked at the

area more carefully, trying to remember how a detective would do this part. And that's when he saw the footprints, lots of them. Footprints other than his own.

They went from the cellar steps over to where the tire tracks ended. Which had to be where the car had parked. Or the truck.

Ted began walking back and forth across the area, his head bent down, looking for clues. Because that's what a detective would do. And something caught his eye, something in the grass near the tire tracks. Something shiny.

A shell casing? From a bullet? Ted gulped, and he knelt down, pushing the grass aside to see better.

But it wasn't a bullet shell reflecting the morning sun. It was the shiny metal band around the eraser at the end of a dark blue wooden pencil. Ted picked it up by the very tip, in case there were fingerprints on it. Because that's how a detective would handle a piece of evidence.

As he slowly turned the pencil, Ted saw what was printed along one side in gold letters: GRANKERSON COUNTY SHERIFF'S OFFICE.

It didn't take a detective to figure out who must have called Deputy Linwood. Only one person other than Ted knew about April and her family. And she had promised not to tell.

Chapter 14

BLAME GAME

By the time he stomped into his classroom on Friday morning, Ted was so angry at Mrs. Mitchell he couldn't even look at her. And he was so fed up with promises that he could hardly say the Pledge of Allegiance. And Ted was so mad at one particular Boy Scout that he was ready to punch himself in the nose.

He wished he had just told Mrs. Mitchell a lie. He should have said he went into the Andersons' driveway because . . . because he saw a crow feather lying on the ground. Something like that. Something simple. A simple lie. Over and done with. Then none of this would have had to happen.

But it did happen. He broke his promise not to tell, and then Mrs. Mitchell broke *her* promise not to tell, and then April and her family got hauled away by Deputy Linwood.

And what gave Mrs. Mitchell the right to be

so nosy? When she'd asked him what he was doing at the Andersons' place, he should have just said, *None of your business, lady.* That's what he should have said, just like that.

After the pledge, Ted stalked over to his sixth-grade command center, ducked under a desk, and sat in his swivel chair. He spun around to his writing desk, yanked out his top secret red notebook, and flipped to where he kept his file about Mrs. Mitchell.

In large letters at the bottom of a page he wrote, "She's a promise breaker. And she can't be trusted. Because she's a liar. And her nose is twenty miles long and it flops around into everybody's business. And her breath smells. Almost all the time. And she's the meanest, ugliest teacher in the whole world!!!!"

When Ted made the fourth exclamation point, he pushed down so hard that he broke the lead of his pencil.

"Ted?"

He swiveled his chair, and there was the evil woman herself, with a big fake smile on her face.

Mrs. Mitchell said, "Are you all right?"

"Fine." Ted didn't look at her, and he didn't *say* the word. He spat it at her.

"Well, you don't look fine. You look upset."

Ted swung his chair around so he faced the windows.

He thought, *I should write my own mystery book. I'm gonna call it* The Case of the Teacher Who Was a Big Fat Liar.

Mrs. Mitchell had never seen Ted like this before. She thought it best to give him some time to cool down.

Speaking to the back of his head, she said, "After I get the fourth graders working on their math, I'd like to have a talk with you, all right?"

She couldn't tell if Ted nodded yes or shook his head no. But Mrs. Mitchell had to hurry over to the fourth-grade corner so she could rescue Hannah, Lizzie, and Keith. Kevin was unbeatable at the word game Boggle, and he tried to force the others to play almost every morning, rattling the wooden letters inside the plastic game cube until the children had to put their hands over their ears.

Ted glared out the window. *She wants to talk to me? Well, I don't want to talk to her. Because it's just going to be a bunch of excuses. Or maybe lies. Yeah, she's probably going to lie. Because once you've told one, it gets easier and easier.*

But it was hard for a boy like Ted to stay furious for long, and ten minutes later, when Mrs. Mitchell asked him to follow her out of room one, he went silently. He was going to listen to what she had to say.

There was a pair of wooden chairs in the hallway, and when they were seated facing each other, Mrs. Mitchell tried to start on a positive note. "I was so glad we talked yesterday and that you were honest with me. It's important to always be honest."

Ted thought, *Oh, this is great. She's talking about being honest? After what she did? What, does she think I'm that stupid? Unbelievable!*

Mrs. Mitchell saw that dark thought pass across Ted's face, but she kept talking, trying to win him over. "Well, I just want you to know that you can talk to me about anything that's bothering you, and it'll stay just between us."

That was too much.

Ted snorted and said, "You mean like the girl and her family at the Anderson farm? You'll keep everything a secret, like *that*?"

Mrs. Mitchell said, "I'm glad you brought that up. We have to talk about them some more."

Ted stood up fast, knocking the chair against the wall. "What's there to talk about? Just . . . just forget about it, okay?"

Mrs. Mitchell said, "Well, it's not that simple. Because of the children. If I—"

Ted cut her off. "You should have thought about *them* before. Because now it's too late."

Mrs. Mitchell shook her head. "I didn't mean—"

"Right," Ted said. "You didn't mean to mess everything up and ruin their lives, but you did. You *did*. And don't try to lie about it. Because I know Deputy Linwood was out there. I saw the tire tracks this morning, on the grass behind the house. And I found this."

Ted held out the blue pencil he'd found. Mrs. Mitchell took it and looked at the lettering, and then she looked into Ted's face and saw the anger and the hurt and the shattered trust.

Ted narrowed his eyes. "And they're gone," he said. "Gone. Thanks to *you*."

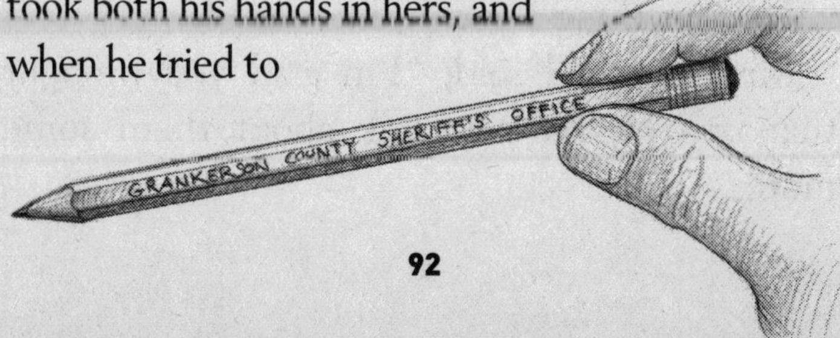

She reached out quickly and took both his hands in hers, and when he tried to pull away, she held on. "Ted, listen to me. I'm so sorry. But you have to hear this. I started feeling like I had to do something last night. Even though I promised you I wouldn't tell anyone. But I wanted to talk to you first. So I didn't do *anything,* and I didn't tell anyone. Not even my husband."

Ted shook his head, as if he hadn't heard right. "What?"

She said it again. "I didn't do anything, and I didn't tell anyone. No one."

Looking into her face, Ted knew Mrs. Mitchell wasn't lying. He just knew. And the mistake he'd made about her cut him to the heart. Not to mention his rotten detective work. Good detectives are suspicious of circumstantial evidence.

He stammered, "I . . . I thought . . . I thought you . . ."

She shook her head. And before Ted could finish his apology, another question took complete control of his thinking, and he said, "Then what happened? Why did the police show up and take them away?"

Mrs. Mitchell said, "I don't know. But I can find out. I'll call Deputy Linwood at lunchtime, and I'll tell you everything I learn, all right?"

Ted wanted to run out the front door of the school and ride his bike over to town hall and make somebody give him the facts, right now.

But he knew he couldn't, so he nodded, and Mrs. Mitchell said, "Then let's get back to class."

Ted opened the door. In one corner Kevin was arguing with Hannah, Lizzie, and Keith, shouting about the best way to find a lowest common denominator. And in the other corner, the eighth graders were passing Carla's iPod from hand to hand, trying to make one pair of earphones work for four pairs of ears.

Mrs. Mitchell had the corners of room one quiet and focused on schoolwork in less than fifteen seconds.

But at the sixth-grade island out in the middle, Ted Hammond was focused on something else. He was thinking like a detective again, a detective who had work to do.

Because this case wasn't closed. Ted felt responsible for April. And her mom and brother, too. He wouldn't feel settled about it until Mrs. Mitchell learned exactly what had happened to them.

Chapter 15

OFFICIAL BUSINESS

When Mrs. Mitchell came out the playground door, Ted pounced.

"What? What did he say?"

Mrs. Mitchell shook her head. "Not much."

It was after-lunch recess, and Ted had been pacing up and down, waiting to hear about his teacher's talk with the police.

Ted frowned. "What do you mean?"

"Leonard—I should say, Deputy Linwood—is being very official today. He wouldn't give me any details. He did say that he had gotten a call about a disturbance at the Anderson place last night, and that he went out there and took care of it. I asked him about the children, and he said 'Official police business. I'm not at liberty to talk about that.' But you were right. He was certainly there."

Ted nodded. "And the family's gone. I saw that myself. But where are they?"

Mrs. Mitchell said, "Well, I'm not sure. Maybe at the social services center in Wheaton. Or maybe they're already on the way to their relatives. But we know that there are good people taking care of them now. And they'll have enough to eat, and everyone will have a safe place to sleep tonight. You can be sure of that. And you can stop worrying about them."

Mrs. Mitchell wasn't quite as sure about that as she sounded. So many things could have happened out at the Andersons' farm last night. But wherever the little family was now, it wasn't right for Ted to keep feeling responsible for them. It was out of his hands, and he needed to let it go.

When Ted didn't say anything, Mrs. Mitchell added, "And you were a big help to them. You really were."

Then she said, "We'll talk again later. . . . I've got to go be the referee before someone gets hurt."

Mrs. Mitchell hurried toward the field where the fourth graders and the eighth graders were playing a lopsided game of kickball.

Ted sat down on the low doorstep.

You were a big help to them. That's what Mrs. Mitchell had said.

Some help I was, he thought. *People you help shouldn't end up being hauled off in a police car. But it wasn't my fault—was it? No. Couldn't be. Mrs. Mitchell didn't squeal, and I didn't tell anyone else. I guess it just happened, that's all. There was a disturbance, and then Deputy Linwood went . . .*

Ted jumped to his feet, his detective mind sparking to life. *"A disturbance"? What does that mean?*

Ted began pacing again. Because in his mystery books, a disturbance that brought the police was usually something scary. Like a gunshot. Or a big fight. Or a fire, or maybe an animal attack. "A disturbance" could mean a lot of things—and none of them were good.

It was great that Mrs. Mitchell had talked to Deputy Linwood. And Ted was glad April and her mom and brother were safe somewhere. But he still wanted to know what had happened on Thursday night out at the Anderson farm.

And that's when Ted decided he needed to go have another look around. A slow look. A careful look. He could go over there tomorrow and give it some time. Now that he wasn't upset. Now that it was just a matter of curiosity.

Because a good detective shouldn't need to ask the police about what happened at the scene of some "official business."

All a detective needed was a good long look at the evidence.

Chapter 16

A LITTLE HOME

The Saturday bundle of the *Omaha World-Tribune* got dropped off before dawn, same as the weekday papers. But all the subscribers in Plattsford, Nebraska, understood that the Saturday paper didn't get delivered until about nine o'clock. Saturday was the day that the paperboy stayed in bed an extra hour or so.

But not this Saturday. Ted was up and out the kitchen door at his regular time. Even though it was the weekend, and even though he could ride out to the Anderson farm anytime he'd finished his chores, he wanted to go before he delivered his papers. He wanted to get there before the clues got any older.

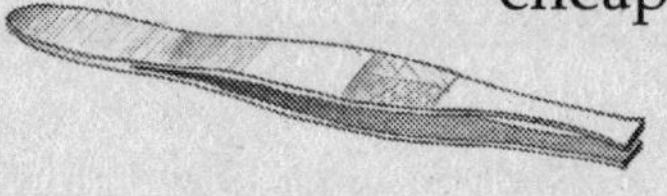

And this time Ted was prepared. He had five or six plastic sandwich bags for collecting evidence, some long tweezers for picking up small clues, a magnifying glass, a cheap plastic camera with nine shots left on the counter, a flashlight, his field notebook, and two freshly sharpened pencils.

Ted noticed something odd before he even got to the house. There was a patch of soft ground next to the mailbox where the driveway crossed the ditch. He'd been expecting to see a set of tire tracks going in toward the farmhouse, and the same tracks coming back out. But it looked like there were tracks from two different kinds of tires. Had there been two cars? Two police cars? Or maybe Deputy Linwood's car had snow tires on the rear wheels and regular tires up front. Hard to say.

Ted pulled out his camera and snapped a picture.

Around back, both basement doors were still wide open, just like on Friday morning. There were a lot of early-morning shadows, so Ted decided to look inside first. The light in the backyard would be better later on.

The flashlight let Ted have his first real look around the basement. He saw the wooden crate he'd almost tripped on. Shining the light in a wide arc, he saw some broken Mason jars, a row of paint cans on rough wooden shelves over near one wall, water and steam pipes hanging overhead, a fuel oil tank, a big furnace, and lots of spiderwebs. The dirt floor gave the place a damp, musty smell.

There wasn't much to investigate, so Ted headed up the stairs.

The kitchen was the way he remembered it—can opener on the counter, empty water jug by the sink. But when he opened the cabinet above the counter, a surprise: Beef stew, soup, instant coffee, Sterno, matches—almost everything he'd brought, all neatly arranged.

But it made sense. You don't stop and bring groceries when the police take you away. Ted thought, *I should take this stuff—after all, I paid for it.* But it seemed like a lot to carry around. Maybe later. He closed the cabinet and went into the living room.

The place was messy, but it looked like Deputy Linwood had given them enough time

to pack up all their things. Ted began a careful search of the living room, but his heart wasn't in it. He wasn't feeling much like a detective. It was more like he was looking for proof that April and her family had actually been here. All he found were six crumpled granola bar wrappers and a small order form for X-Men T-shirts, something Artie must have torn out of a comic book.

On the stairs going to the second floor Ted saw footprints in the dust. He stepped on the first few treads to be sure they felt solid and then walked up.

Some kids had been in the house, probably right after the Andersons moved. All the closet doors were open, and there were shoe boxes and newspapers and coat hangers scattered across the floors, along with some broken bottles. Someone had written and drawn pictures with black and red spray paint all over the walls in the bedrooms. It made the place feel creepy, sort of dangerous. Ted thought, *No wonder April and her family stayed downstairs.* He would have left right then, but the upper windows weren't boarded up, so the morning sunlight made the rooms feel almost cheerful, in spite of the vandalism.

Ted had an idea, and he went to the front bedroom. He was looking for something. And there in front of the window on the right, he saw fresh footprints in the dust. He snapped a photo. Those had to be April's footprints, right in front of the window where he had first seen her face. And he thought, *That was less than a week ago*. It seemed much longer.

There was a closed door in the hallway, and when Ted opened it, he saw a set of narrow steps going up to the attic. And again, there were footprints in the dust.

The attic was another surprise. It looked like the Andersons had left almost everything they had stored up there. Ted could see why. Most of the stuff was in bad shape. Three wicker-bottom chairs with tattered seats, a broken iron bed frame, stacks of empty cardboard boxes, a painted dresser with a split top, a broken mirror on its own wooden stand, two big steamer trunks with the leather straps chewed to bits by the mice, a wooden baby cradle with a missing rocker. Almost everything he saw was broken or damaged in some way, but it still made him feel like he was looking at a family's history.

Standing in the center under the peak of the roof, Ted looked toward one end of the room, and then toward the other. And that's when he noticed something unusual. Amid all the dusty rummage and the cobwebs loaded with dead flies and moths, the window facing the northwest was spotless, perfectly clean.

Ted went closer, watching his step on the loose floorboards. Someone had pulled a sagging armchair in front of the window. On the floor to one side he saw some dirty rags, the ones used to clean the glass. And Ted knew instantly what they were. Little blue pajamas and some tiny T-shirts—baby clothes. From the two bags downstairs in the living room.

On one arm of the chair was a book, an old one: *Little Women* by Louisa May Alcott. Looking at the footprints in the dust, Ted could tell which cardboard box it had been taken from.

He picked up the book and sniffed it. Old.

His mom had some books like this, and the paper had a special smell. Ted saw a bookmark, and when he opened the brittle yellow pages, it fluttered to the floor. It was a folded Snickers wrapper.

Ted suddenly knew where he was. He was in April's hideout, the place she came to be by herself. A place she had cleaned and dusted. A quiet place, with a beautiful view out across the prairie. April had made herself a little home.

Ted sat down, and as he looked out the attic window, he saw how April had seen him coming, that first afternoon when he'd tried to sneak up close. Over the roof of the barn he could still see the path he had left as he'd walked through the long grass.

He would have had a hard time putting it into words, but sitting there with her book in his hands, looking out the window she had cleaned, Ted felt like he and April could have become friends. Maybe they already had.

He leaned over, picked up the folded candy wrapper, and tucked it back between the pages. And as he put the book into his shoulder bag, Ted wished that he'd had a chance to say good-bye.

Chapter 17

LIFE GOES ON

Monday and Tuesday felt dull and ordinary to Ted. Up at six thirty. Eat. Get the papers. Deliver the papers. Ride to school. Say the Pledge. Read. Review the homework. Listen to Mrs. Mitchell. Begin the new schoolwork. Eat. Play outside. Read. Ride home. Do chores. Eat. Do homework. Read. Sleep.

The quiet little town of Plattsford, Nebraska, was back to its same old self again, and for the first time in Ted's life, the place seemed sort of slow and boring to him.

Ted got a new mystery at the library on Monday afternoon, and it had a great title: *The Blood Runs Cold*. But the plot? Routine. Predictable. After the real-life events of the week before, the story seemed pale and thin.

To be fair, other local mysteries were still bubbling, still needing to be solved. At the beginning of the week, every home in Plattsford had gotten a letter from the Wheaton school board. The superintendent explained that with so few students next year, it seemed likely that Red Prairie Learning Center would have to close.

That letter caused a stir at Ted's dinner table on Tuesday.

His dad said, "It's a bad sign, the school closin' down. Market'll be next, an' then we'll have to drive thirty miles just to get groceries."

Ted's big brother speared a piece of meat on his plate and said, "'Bout time this town died."

His mom snapped, "Lucas Hammond, you take that back!" She was furious. "After all the hard work that's gone into giving you a good place to grow up, and you say something like that!"

Lucas had one more year of high school, and everyone knew he wasn't going to stay on the family farm one minute longer than he had to. Lucas was going to the University of Nebraska, and after college, he'd made it clear that he was headed for someplace that had wide sidewalks and tall buildings, restaurants and taxicabs. And, over time, his dad had accepted that. You can't force someone to become a farmer.

Ted and his sister Sharon waited for the

secondary explosion. But it didn't come. Their dad finished the bite he was chewing, swallowed, took a sip of coffee, and said, "Everybody's entitled to his own opinions."

And after a short silence, the talk turned to news about Sharon's class trip at the end of May to Washington, D.C.

Sharon wasn't interested in farm life either. But Ted? Ted was going to stay. He knew it, and so did his dad.

When Ted's 4-H adviser had come by one Saturday in April to give him some pointers about grooming his calf for the local 4-H competition, afterward he had told Ted's dad, "Looks like you've got yourself a cattleman there."

And John Hammond had smiled and said, "One kid out of three ain't great, but it'll do."

Still, it's hard to have a farm without a town nearby, and it's hard to have a town without a school. So a lot of people in Plattsford were thinking and talking about the future of Red Prairie Learning Center.

Did Ted like the idea that his school might close? No, but there was no point in worrying about it. Did Ted like the idea that he might have to sit on a school bus for two hours a day next year? No, but it wasn't his decision. And would the town survive if room one suddenly went silent? As far as Ted could see, only time would solve *that* mystery.

A couple of times on Sunday, and once on Monday, Ted had almost told his mom how he'd discovered this homeless family, and how he'd given them some food. He had to tell her, because he had to pay for the things he'd borrowed. But it felt too soon. He still wanted to keep the story to himself.

Riding past the Anderson farm to get his newspapers on Monday morning, and then again on Tuesday, Ted wondered about April and her family. He thought about them off and on during school, sitting inside his pentagon of desks in room one. And he also thought about them at night when he turned off the light and tried to sleep. He couldn't help it. Were they in Wheaton? Or maybe in Lincoln somewhere? Or had the authorities really been able to help them get all the way to their relatives in Colorado?

Ted had no idea, and it bothered him not to know.

So as he rode home from school on Wednesday, Ted decided to go straight down Main Street, hop off his bike, and walk right into town hall—which had recently moved into a former insurance office.

Because Ted thought if he asked the right person the right questions, maybe he could get some real information about April. And her mom and brother. What could be the harm in that?

Ted pedaled faster, thinking of all the questions he was going to ask.

As much as his head wanted him to hurry to town hall, Ted's stomach wanted him to stop—for an after-school snack. Just a little one. It would only take a few minutes. After all, the E&A Market was right on the way to town hall.

So Ted listened to his stomach, and he stopped.

In books about how to solve mysteries, nowhere does it say that a detective ought to listen to his stomach. But maybe it should. Because Ted's stomach was about to lead him to some vital information.

Chapter 18

BIG NEWS

All the eighth graders in room one thought the fourth-grade kids were funny, even cute. And they all got a big kick out of Kevin—who was probably smarter than any three of them combined.

But the four big kids didn't have much use for the one sixth grader in room one. They barely noticed him. Maybe they needed to feel like they were so far beyond sixth grade. Maybe they thought they were so much older, so much more mature. Whatever the reason, the eighth graders basically ignored Ted, especially when all four of them were together—which was almost always.

However, when Ted happened to catch one eighth grader alone, it wasn't so bad. Of all the eighth graders, Josh was the one most willing to be friendly toward a lowly sixth grader. And, as Ted was buying a bottle of root beer and a

Slim Jim sausage at the E&A Market on Wednesday afternoon, Josh was in line right behind him, buying exactly the same snack.

So they both sat on the bench in front of the store, unscrewed the caps of their twenty-ounce bottles, and on a silent signal, began guzzling to see who could drink the most before stopping.

Josh won. And after a terrific burp that made Mrs. Gorsley on the other side of the street stop and frown at him, he said, "So, di'juh hear about what happened at the Anderson farm the other night?"

Ted almost blew root beer out of his nose. But he tried to act cool. After all, Plattsford was a very small town. It was entirely possible that the news about April and her family had spread to everyone.

Ted nodded. "Yeah, I heard."

Josh ripped the end off the Slim Jim wrapper, took a big bite, started chewing, and leaned in closer. "Well listen to this—I found out the girl might get sent to juvie. Been in trouble before."

Ted stared. "R-really?"

Josh nodded, "Yeah, big-time. Fighting at school, shoplifting, stuff like that." To underline this point, Josh shot a big wad of spit onto the sidewalk. He wiped his chin and said, "Yeah, I heard all about it from my brother."

"From your brother?" Ted said.

"Yeah, Jimmy. He's at the high school, same grade as your sister. Who I think is very *nice,* by the way. The news is all over Wheaton High."

Ted shook his head. The information was coming too fast. He felt like he was having trouble hearing.

He said, "But what . . . what actually happened? At the Anderson place?"

Josh took another bite of sausage. He enjoyed seeing how Ted was so impressed. "Yeah, well, it was like these five kids from Wheaton, and they were out, driving around, like after they went to a movie. And they drove in the driveway at the farm, and somebody saw the car. Called the cops. So they all got *busted.* And one of their dads had left some bottles in the trunk and everything. That's what the kids told the cops—yeah, *right.* Classic."

Ted felt like he was in some science fiction movie where everything shifts to slow motion. *What Josh just said—he's . . . he's not talking about April. It's . . . it's some high school girl who's in trouble . . . it's not April!*

Josh spat again, got up, stretched, and said, "Hey, I'll see y'around, okay? And say hi to your sister for me. And you can tell her I think that she is very *nice*."

Ted sat on the bench, almost in a daze, sorting and sifting and processing this massive chunk of new data. Because if catching those high school kids was the "official business" that Deputy Linwood wouldn't tell Mrs. Mitchell about . . . then something *else* must have happened to April. And Alexa and Artie.

Because they were definitely gone.

Ted tried to picture the scene that night. First, the noisy high school kids came, and then the police arrived, probably with flashing lights. And there must have been a lot of shouting.

And Ted could imagine Alexa getting scared. Because maybe the high school kids had started to come into the house. Or even the police. Alexa and April and Artie must have been scared out of their minds. And then the police and the kids left. And then the three of them must have packed up and left too. Because they wouldn't have felt safe at the Anderson place anymore, not safe at all.

Then Ted had a terrible thought: *Maybe*

April thought the police came because of me!

But he knew he was just guessing, about all of it.

Only one thing was for sure: A mom and her two kids had left the Andersons' farmhouse late last Thursday night. In a hurry.

Ted tossed his empty root beer bottle into a trash can, stuck the Slim Jim into his back pocket, and jumped onto his bike.

April and Artie and Alexa could be anywhere by now, but Ted knew exactly where they had started from. And when. So he had to take this new information and go out there right now and look around for clues.

Again.

Chapter 19

NOT MANY WORDS

Ted felt stupid.

He had left the E&A Market and pedaled out to the farm at top speed, not caring if anybody saw him. He had arrived out of breath, rushed into the house, looked up and down and all around. He had turned over every object in the living room, examined the whole attic, poked through each bedroom, scoured the backyard, and even went through the barn.

Then he'd gone back into the house for another walk-through, and he'd looked everywhere again. And all the while, Ted had tried to think like Alexa. He had tried to imagine what plan might have popped into her frightened mind after the police left on Thursday night.

And at the end of thirty-three minutes, what did the great young detective have to show for all the work he had done? Zilch. Zero. Zip.

Ted had found nothing, discovered nothing, learned nothing.

And after this desperate hunt for new clues, Ted had sat on the arm of the reclining chair for almost five minutes, and he had made himself review everything he knew. And all the facts had led right back to where he sat, looking around the cluttered front room in the Andersons' farmhouse. He felt like he had reached the end of the road.

Ted stood up and walked slowly into the kitchen, defeated, headed for the basement stairs, headed for his bike out in the yard, headed for home. But when he had his hand on the knob of the cellar door, he stopped and stared at the kitchen counter.

And that's when Ted felt *really* stupid.

Because in all his rushing about, he had missed an important clue. Something he should have seen, something so easy to spot—actually, to *not* spot. Because something was missing.

Two days ago the can opener he'd bought had been in the kitchen, lying right there on the counter. And now it wasn't. And over by the sink? The empty water jug was also gone.

Ted stepped quickly to the counter, reached up, and pulled open the cabinet doors.

The Sterno cans, the instant coffee, the matches, the stew, the bread, soup, everything. Gone.

Ted stared at the red and white checked paper that lined the bottom shelf, and he began running through the possibilities. *Could have been some bums came by and cleaned the place out. Could have been more high school kids sneaking in and stealing everything. Could have been . . .*

He stopped thinking. He almost stopped breathing. The faded paper had been covering that bottom shelf for many years. It was stuck down flat. But in one place, over on the right side, it was puckered. In that one place, the paper had been peeled up, and then pushed back down. And sticking out from under the front edge of the shelf liner, Ted saw a small piece of dark brown paper—just a corner.

He got hold of that corner and pulled. It slid

right out. A Snickers wrapper had been opened flat, and then carefully creased into a rectangle.

The thin plastic crinkled as Ted unfolded it.

Someone had written on the inside of the wrapper. With a blue ballpoint pen. In neat, round, flowing cursive. Not many words.

The first few made a short sentence.

We're close.

The last word was the name of a month. And a girl.

April

Chapter 20

SECOND CHANCE

"'We're close,'" Ted whispered. Then he wondered, *How close?*

And standing there in the kitchen, the answer came almost instantly. April had to be staying close enough to walk to the Anderson place, get the supplies, and then walk back. And do that without going through town. Or being seen.

Close by. That meant another empty house. And Ted knew there were two other abandoned farmhouses, both less than a mile away, one east along Route 2 and one to the west. They must have gone to one or the other.

But which one?

Ted made himself think logically. The family had arrived at night, and they had come from the east on Route 2, so they had gone right past one of the empty houses, the one to the east. But there wouldn't have been any lights on, and the house sat back pretty far from the road. They couldn't have seen it.

An idea flashed into Ted's mind, and he rushed from the kitchen, dashed through the front room, ran up the stairs to the second floor, and then right on up into the attic. He hurried to April's window and bent down to examine the wooden frame of the bottom sash. He was panting so hard that his breath made foggy patches on the glass.

Yes—fingerprints in the dust. And the bent nails that had held the window shut? They'd been turned to the side, out of the way. And the side tracks above the sash? Fresh scrape marks on the darkened wood. And on the floor below the window, a piece of wood, the perfect length to use as a prop.

This window had been opened. Recently.

Then Ted lifted the sash and used the short board to hold it up. And he put his head out and looked to his left. Toward the west.

There it was, the Kosczinski farm, plain as could be, looking deserted and overgrown. And not very far away.

Ted smiled. It wasn't Alexa who had worked out an emergency exit plan in case the family

needed one. It was April. She had spotted another hideaway, right down the road, just by looking out her own little window.

Ted was sure all three of them were in that other farmhouse, right now. He would have bet his whole savings account on it.

And from his perch high above the prairie, watching the afternoon sun throw long shadows across the land, Ted felt like he was being given a second chance. A chance to do things right. To really help.

April wanted him to find her. And her family. That's why she'd left the note. Hoping that he would find it. And he did find it.

And April had known he would still want to help. And he did want to.

But what kind of help did they need?

Sure, he could sneak some more food to them. But that would be like trying to fix a broken fence post with duct tape. These people needed a major repair job. They needed . . . they needed . . . *everything*.

Their problems seemed so huge, so complicated to Ted. And finding a solution seemed so far beyond his own skills and talents and experience. Because Ted saw that this wasn't like reading a mystery book, where he could stop in the middle, and take his time, and try to guess the ending. And if he didn't get it right, it didn't matter. In a book, the ending was already settled, all figured out, waiting for him in the last chapter. With a book, all he ever had to do was keep reading.

No, this wasn't like figuring out a mystery novel. It was like figuring out . . . life. Real life.

And Ted was smart enough to see that there had to be a real-life solution. Something that would help these people. Permanently.

He tried again to put himself in April's place, but he couldn't imagine what that would be like. Your dad, suddenly gone? Leaving your town and your school and your friends? She had lost so much. They all had.

Ted felt helpless. But he knew that wasn't right. The Boy Scout motto is Be Prepared. It's not Be Depressed.

Still, Ted didn't feel prepared at all, not for this.

He shut the attic window, made his way over to the stairs, and started down, feeling less certain with each step. By the time he'd walked all the way down into the dark, damp cellar, he felt like a total failure—a lousy detective, an unprepared Boy Scout, a bad friend.

It's the kind of moment that tests a person's character.

To Ted's credit, as he walked up the bulkhead steps into the afternoon sunlight, he let go of something. It wasn't easy, but he let go of his pride—that feeling that he had to do all this on his own, that *he* had to be the superdetective, the great helper, the lone hero.

And right out loud, he said, "What I need is help. I need help with this—*lots* of help."

Riding back into town, Ted felt so good about his decision. And he also remembered that teamwork is important. Even for the one and only sixth grader. And for a Boy Scout.

And for a detective, too. After all, Sherlock Holmes got help from Professor Watson now and then, right? And the Hardy Boys *always* worked together.

By the time he got to Main Street, Ted had

already chosen his assistant, the perfect person to help him out. It was someone he could trust, someone with experience, someone who knew how important it was to keep a promise.

And it didn't even matter that this person's nose was twenty miles long.

Chapter 21

POSSIBILITY

"And you're *sure* that's where they are?"

Ted didn't like the tone of Mrs. Mitchell's question. An assistant wasn't supposed to doubt and challenge every single detail that the team leader presented.

After he had decided to get some help, Ted had ridden his bike straight back to the school. Mrs. Mitchell was still in the classroom, grading the Civil War reports the eighth graders had turned in. Ted had told Mrs. Mitchell his news, he had asked for her help, and now he was sitting in a chair in front of her desk and she was asking all these annoying questions.

Ted said, "I'm not *completely* sure they're at the Kosczinski place. But that's where I'd be if I was them."

"You mean, 'If I *were* them,'" Mrs. Mitchell said.

Having a teacher for an assistant had some

serious drawbacks. Grammar corrections was one of them. She had also given Ted a lot of bad news about all the problems April and her family might have with the law, and maybe with the child welfare people, too.

But Ted tried to keep focused on his mission.

"I'm going to find out if they're there for sure tomorrow morning. But if they *are* there, then what do you think we can do? That's what I want to know. Because it's like they're stuck. And I don't see why they don't just hitch a ride back to Texas, or maybe rent a car. Or walk into town and make a phone call to somebody in Colorado. I don't get it."

Mrs. Mitchell said, "From what you've told me, I think April's mom is feeling too scared and upset. She's the one who needs help the most. Her husband's gone, she's worried about a man she doesn't like, she's worried about her children, about the future. She's afraid to go back, and she's afraid to go forward. Poor thing."

Ted said, "When she gave me five dollars for groceries, April's mom said she had money. At the ATM. Do you think that's true? I mean, why act like you're homeless if you have money? I don't get that, either."

Mrs. Mitchell nodded. "It's hard to understand, but I've read about people who get hit all of a sudden with big problems. Sometimes they try to run away from them. And when you feel that way, it doesn't matter if you have money or not."

They were both quiet a moment.

Then Ted said, "So my question's still the same: Do you think there's a way to really help? What do they need?"

Mrs. Mitchell paused. She said, "I think they need what everybody needs. A safe place to raise a family. A school. A place to worship. A place to work. A grocery store. It's not complicated. But it's not easy, either. They just need a place to live. A home."

Ted brightened. "You mean, like right here, in Plattsford?"

Mrs. Mitchell shook her head. "No, I didn't mean that. Every place is different, but they're all pretty much the same, too. No, they've got to move on and find their own home. And we ought to be able to help with that. If they're where you think they are."

Ted didn't want to let go of his idea. "But

their home *could* be here, couldn't it? I mean, if they wanted?"

"Well," Mrs. Mitchell said, "it's more complicated than that."

Ted held on. "But you just said it's *not* complicated. You said, 'It's not easy, but it's not complicated'—something like that. So that means it's not *impossible* . . . right? This *could* be where they live—right?"

"Well, I guess so. I mean, it's not impossible," Mrs. Mitchell said. "Nothing's impossible. But . . ."

"Okay," Ted said, "I'll tell you what."

He felt like it was time to take charge of this project, be the team leader, and let the assistant assist, like she was supposed to. He stood up and said, "Tomorrow I'll find out if they're really there, where I think they are, and then we'll see what's possible. Or what isn't. But I'm late for my chores, so I've got to go."

He hurried to the door. "Thanks, Mrs. Mitchell. Great ideas. Really. See you tomorrow."

He was gone, and Mrs. Mitchell didn't know whether to smile or frown. So she did both, first one, then the other. And then she went back to grading the last report on the Civil War.

Ted didn't have a problem choosing whether to smile or frown.

He liked his new idea. A lot. It grabbed hold of his imagination—first his mind, and then his heart.

Even though he was going to get yelled at because he was late for chores, Ted smiled all the way home.

Chapter 22

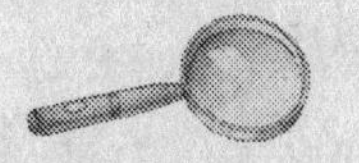

QUESTIONS

Ted thought about April and her family as he rushed through his Wednesday afternoon chores. He also thought about his town, about Plattsford, Nebraska.

In his mind, Ted rode along his whole paper route, taking note of all the houses, Clara's Diner, the town offices, the boarded-up storefronts, the grocery store, and all the people.

He also thought about his school, about room one, about Mrs. Mitchell and all the students, including himself.

And at the dinner table Ted decided to ask a question—a test question.

He looked at his mom and said, "You know how we hear about huge disasters on the news? Well, if there were these people, and they lost everything they had, like in a hurricane or an earthquake, and some of them came to our town, do you think people here would try to help them?"

She nodded. "Why, sure they would. Look at what happened with that big thunderstorm two years ago August, when it lifted the roof right off the Thompsons' house? The very next day that family had a place to stay, they had help fixing their house, they had help with getting their winter wheat crop planted. They had more help than they knew what to do with."

Ted said, "But the Thompsons are neighbors. What about strangers?"

"Shouldn't make any difference. People here are good about helping out. If you can, you help."

So far, so good. Ted decided to push the test a little further.

He said, "So, like, if two or three people needed a place to stay, and everywhere else was filled up, you'd let them stay here awhile? Right here at our farm?"

And his mom said, "Well why not, for goodness' sake? We've got a whole extra room upstairs that I only use for sewing now and then, and we've got the old bunkhouse where the hired hands used to stay. We could take care of six or seven people, if we had to. And we could feed them too, couldn't we, John?"

Ted's dad made a face at the thought of that many more mouths to feed, but he nodded and said, "For a while. If we had to."

In his room a half hour later, Ted felt encouraged by what his mom had said. But he still had a lot of unanswered questions. And one question sat at the top of his list: *Are April and her family still here*?

Because if they *weren't* where he thought they were, if they weren't close anymore like April had said in her note, then that would be the end of it.

But if they *were* in town, Ted was going to do his best to try to make them feel right at home.

Chapter 23

INVITATION

It was a rainy morning, so Ted had to wear his rain suit: jacket, pants, and a hood with a long visor. The rain gear made bike riding a hot and sticky business. Ted would have much rather been wet with rain instead of sweat. But his mom insisted. The bright yellow plastic kept the rain off, and it helped drivers see her son more clearly. The rain suit made Mrs. Hammond feel good. It made Ted feel like a giant goldfinch.

Besides, this was one morning he didn't want to be visible from half a mile away.

When Ted reached the junction of County Road 7 and Route 2, he didn't stop and pick up his bundle of newspapers. He was going to do that on the way back. Besides, his shoulder bag was loaded.

He had made a predawn raid on the kitchen—three cans of soup, a plastic bag of dinner rolls, six oatmeal raisin cookies, and a two-liter soda bottle he had washed out and filled up with milk. Because if April and Artie and Alexa were still around, they probably needed more food.

Ted turned right onto the state highway and pedaled the last half mile as quickly as he could, glad to see that the rain was stopping.

His mom and dad had known the Kosczinski family, but Ted had never met them. Their place had been empty a lot longer than the Anderson farm.

When the highway was clear of traffic, Ted turned off into the long, curving driveway. It was lined with a windbreak of scraggly cedar trees, which was good. They blocked the view from the highway and gave Ted some cover as he approached the house.

The roof of the wide front porch was sagging, and the wooden siding that had once been white was weathered and gray. Half a dozen bricks from the chimney lay scattered across the upper roof, and large patches of shingles had been blown away. The front door and the first-floor windows were boarded over, but not fully covered. A lot of the second-floor windows were broken, probably by rocks.

Behind the house and to the left, one side of the main barn was caved in. A ragged fence line limped toward the barn, posts leaning every which way, all covered with tangled vines and rusty barbed wire.

The whole place looked dismal and unfriendly, and Ted almost wished April and her family weren't here.

But they were.

As he walked his bike around the back corner of the house, Ted inspected a patch of rain-softened ground. And he saw clear footprints—April's sneakers, the same footprints he'd seen in the dust inside the Andersons' house.

And when he looked up, there she was, looking out at him through a big rip in the back screen door. She was wearing the NASCAR shirt again.

April gave him a little wave and half a smile, but when Ted said, "Hey!," she shook her head and put a finger to her lips.

After he tiptoed up onto the back porch, she

whispered, "I don't want Mama to know you're here. I've been watchin' you get your newspapers every morning from an upstairs window. Took ya awhile to find us."

Ted nodded. "I thought you were gone. And I even thought it was my fault. That last day I left? My teacher was driving past, and she saw me, and . . . and I had to tell her about you."

April's face darkened, so Ted rushed ahead. "But I made her promise not to tell anybody, and she didn't. She didn't. She could have, and I know she felt like she ought to, but she didn't. She's okay. Really. And that's not why the police came. It was some high school kids came out there. But you probably figured that out."

She shook her head. "We didn't know anything. One second we're all asleep, and then there's all these voices and flashin' lights. We hid out upstairs in a closet. And when it got quiet, we came here. It was bad. And my mom's still upset. But I can work it out. And Artie's bein' more help than he was. We're goin' as soon as we can. As soon as my mom can handle it. I'm gonna work it out."

All this was said in whispers, with the torn screen door between them.

And the second time April said she was going to work it out, Ted thought, *She's like me. She's trying to do everything herself.*

As if he had known it all his life, instead of for less than one day, Ted said, "Y' know, it's okay to get help when you need it. And you need help. 'Specially your mom."

She hissed, "There's nothin' wrong with her."

"I know that. But she—"

"We don't need any help."

Ted said, "Then why'd you leave me that note? In the other house?"

"Food," April said, with a toss of her head. "We just needed food."

"Fine—here," and Ted unloaded his shoulder bag. "You can tell your mom you found all this lying on the back steps. And don't bother saying thank you. Don't want you to feel obliged. Since you don't need any help." He pulled something else from his bag and set it down next to the soup. "And you might as well keep this, too." It was the old copy of *Little Women*, carefully wrapped in plastic to keep it dry.

Ted was all the way back at his bicycle before April caught up to him. He spun around, and she said, "I just . . . I just don't know what I ought to do. I just . . . don't."

Ted said, "Well, me neither—not exactly. But if you want, I can tell you one thing for sure."

April nodded, and Ted said, "I know for sure that you and your mom and brother have to get out of here right away. And into a real house, someplace where you can stay like visitors. Otherwise your mom'll get into trouble. Because of you and Artie, mostly. Parents aren't allowed to keep kids out of school, or keep kids in a house with no plumbing or electricity or anything. It's against the law. They'll take both of you away from her. Mrs. Mitchell said so. And I believe her. She knows about stuff like that."

April nodded slowly as Ted talked. She kept a brave face on, but Ted was pretty sure she was scared, to have the problem laid out like a fish on a skinning board. It scared him, too.

In a small voice, April said, "So . . . you've got an idea?"

Ted did have an idea, but it had changed three times just in the last hour. He went with his newest concept.

"My idea is that I come out here later with my mom, just me and my mom in our van. Your mom knows me, and she'll like my mom. And my mom'll invite your mom and her family to come and stay at our place for a few days."

April shook her head. "She won't want to do that."

Ted said, "She'll be okay, once she sees how people want to help."

April said, "People wanted to help us back in Texas, too—from the army. Family assistance people. Mama didn't like it when they came. Always ended up crying. And then she packed us up and took off."

Ted said, "But this won't be like an army visit. It'll be a mom talking to another mom."

"Well, *my* mom'll want to run off if I tell her you're comin'. Then what?"

Ted shrugged. "Don't let her. Make her stay. You and Artie. Tell her that both of you really want to go and stay at the Hammonds'. For a visit."

"You mean, say no to my mom? You don't know her. She'll get mad."

Ted felt like he had to be tough, almost mean. "Who cares if she gets mad, as long as she gets helped? Because she *needs* help. That's what my teacher says. So she can stop being scared. Because she doesn't have to be scared, not about anything." Ted thought a second, then said, "Maybe you shouldn't tell her we're coming. My mom and I'll just show up. But you do whatever you think's best."

April looked back toward the door, and then said, "You better go now. She's gonna wake up soon. So . . . when're you comin' back?"

Pulling a time out of thin air, Ted said, "About . . . four o'clock. Just me and my mom."

April made a face like she'd stubbed a toe. "And you're *sure* I've got to do this?"

"I'm sure you've got to do *something*. That's all I'm sure about. And this makes more sense than anything else I can think of."

April shrugged. "Then I guess we've got to try it."

"Yeah," said Ted, "we do." He bent down and picked up his bike. "Have a good day, okay?"

"Won't be easy," she said. "Thank you for the food. And the book."

And as Ted got to the corner of the house, April called softly, "Hey, you were right about the pump. At the other place. Works great now. 'Bye."

Ted smiled over his shoulder and waved. And at that moment he wished with all his heart that he didn't look like a giant goldfinch. On a bicycle.

Chapter 24

MYSTERY-PROOF

Ted was tired of thinking. He felt like his thinker needed a day off. Or a month. Maybe a year. And it was only nine thirty in the morning.

He had been sitting at his writing desk ever since the Pledge of Allegiance, thinking and thinking and thinking. About what he'd said to April earlier. About how he was going to help her, and her mom, and her brother.

Ted had already chewed the erasers off of three new pencils, and he had covered two pages in a spiral notebook with aimless doodling. Thinking and thinking and thinking.

Because so many things had to happen before four o'clock this afternoon.

Like asking his mom if three homeless people could come and visit for a while. Oh, and would you take off early from work so you can be home in time to drive to the Kosczinski place and convince a frightened lady to get in the van with us? And, yes, all three of them are staying for dinner. And overnight. And none of them have had a shower or a bath in at least a week, maybe two.

Ted hadn't even worked up the courage to talk to Mrs. Mitchell yet. Because he had things he needed her to do too. Gratefully, she'd been busy for the last half hour, arguing with the eighth graders about the scores she had given them on their Civil War reports.

As Ted sat there, pencil in his hand, trying to avoid thinking about April and his mom and Mrs. Mitchell, his eye landed on the book he had finished over the weekend, *The Blood Runs Cold*. It was right there on the corner of the desk.

And Ted asked himself, *Why do I like mysteries so much?*

And since he had his pencil handy, he flipped to a clean sheet of paper in his notebook and he wrote that very question at the top of the page:

Why do I like mysteries so much?

And then he tried to think some more. So he could write down every reason he could think of.

And he thought, *Look at me—I'm so crazy that I'm trying to solve the mystery of why I like mysteries so much!*

But crazy or not, Ted actually wanted to know, so he began writing out the reasons.

1. I like the action and the suspense of a mystery.
2. I like seeing how the detectives think about the clues.
3. I like how everything works out in the end.
4. I like it when the detectives outsmart the bad guys.
5. I like to figure out the solution before the story ends.

Ted felt like he could keep finding more reasons, but he knew he was only trying to avoid thinking about April's problem. And his own problems. Which were related to April's problem.

And at that moment, it struck him: Today—this whole day—it's like a mystery!

But it wasn't, not really. Because most mysteries started with something bad that's already happened, or that's about to happen. And the mystery is, how did it happen, and whose fault is it? Start with a bad thing, and figure out how it happened, or who did it.

For today's events, Ted wanted no mystery at all. Zero suspense. He wanted everything to work out just right.

So he thought, *I guess what I need today is an antimystery.*

Because he wanted this day to be mystery-proofed. Ted wanted nothing bad, nothing unexpected, not one single scary, uncertain moment.

But how? he thought. *How could I ever make that happen?*

And there he was once again, thinking and thinking and thinking.

Except this time, he got results.

Ted knew he couldn't really bad-proof the whole day. But in a flash he realized there was one way to come very close. He could at least give himself a fighting chance to end up with a mystery-free day.

It was simple, and he already knew that it worked, and he had even proved it before.

To mystery-proof a day, a week, maybe even a whole life, Ted needed one simple idea, just two words: Be Prepared.

The *idea* was so basic, so clear.

Ted was pretty sure that the hard part would be the *doing*.

Chapter 25

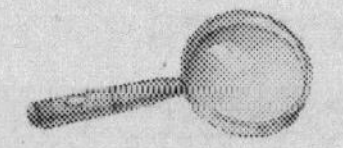

THE DOING

"You *promised* this girl I was going to do *what*? At four o'clock? *Today*?"

It was ten thirty Thursday morning, and Ted had borrowed Mrs. Mitchell's office phone for the first part of his preparations, the talking-to-his-mom part. He was glad that she was in Wheaton, and he was in Plattsford. His mom worked at a bank three days a week, and her desk was right out in the lobby. So that helped to keep her from yelling too loud.

And after the shock had worn off, and after Ted had told her all the details of the little family's story, Katherine Hammond warmed right up. "Those poor dears," she said. "What they must have been through!"

And because his mom was a decent detective herself, she said, "Say—*you're* the one who's been taking food from the pantry, to give to those people, right?"

"Right," Ted admitted, "but I've got a record of everything, and I'm paying for all of it." It's hard to be mad about kindness. And so the first part of his preparation was finished.

Twenty minutes later Ted had completed all the other calls on his list. And he'd gotten a positive, enthusiastic response from everybody.

He felt like this thing was coming together. And it seemed like the hard part wasn't the doing after all. The hard part had been figuring out what the doing ought to be.

What Ted didn't know was that after he had made his one phone call to his mom, she had then made four phone calls. Because once she had bought into Ted's plan, she needed to make some preparations of her own.

And Ted also didn't know that after he'd made his one phone call to Delmar Breslin, the town manager, Delmar had made six other calls of his own. Plus he'd walked across the street to talk to his friends at the American Legion post.

And after Ted had called Clara at the diner, and Mr. Dawcey at the feed store, and Mr. Jackson at the used car lot, and Mrs. Albright at the bank, and Deputy Sheriff Linwood at the town hall, and Pastor Ablom at the Lutheran church, all of these people had made phone calls and visits and run errands of their own. And some of them had also sent e-mails, and some of them had even given a few orders.

There wasn't much time, and everyone in town wanted to be prepared.

Chapter 26

MAIN STREET

It was four fifteen on a Thursday afternoon in May, but on Main Street in Plattsford, Nebraska, it looked like the Fourth of July. Except there were more people, close to three hundred. Because news of how this struggling little town was planning to welcome a fallen soldier's family had fanned out across the prairie like a wildfire.

At the start of Main Street near the county road, a canvas banner, forty feet long with letters two feet high, was stretched from side to side:

WELCOME, THAYER FAMILY—
OUR HOME IS YOUR HOME

That had been one of Delmar Breslin's ideas, one of about ten. As the town manager, he saw a huge opportunity in this event to develop some town spirit in a town that sorely needed some. It was also his idea to have the reporter for the county newspaper, the *Weekly Observer*, on hand to snap some pictures of him and the town council. And the brave army family, too, of course.

And it had been the newspaper reporter's idea to call his friend Annie Mason. She shot video footage for KETV in Omaha now and then. She drove the forty-five miles from Wheaton because it seemed like a natural human interest story.

Annie Mason was so glad she'd made the effort. The banner, the people lining both sides of the street, the waving flags, the Wheaton High School Marching Band playing "The Stars and Stripes Forever," she loved it all. As she walked around with her smallest digital camera—the one that didn't make people feel self-conscious—she felt like she was capturing a wonderful slice of everything that was good about small-town America. And to see support for the troops expressed this way, as kindness for the family left behind, well, it was great documentary footage.

She got this terrific image of the used-car salesman grinning from ear to ear as he held up his sign in front of a shiny red Dodge:

A GENUINE AMERICAN CAR
DONATED BY JACKSON'S QUALITY MOTORS
FOR THE EXCLUSIVE USE OF THE THAYER FAMILY
FOR AS LONG AS THEY NEED IT!

Annie talked to Clara on the sidewalk in front of the diner with her name on it. Clara was selling—you guessed it—apple pie, at twenty-five cents a slice. Demand was high, and the woman laughed and joked with the customers lined up three deep around her table.

The short interview with the schoolteacher and her students, that was Annie's favorite bit so far. The kids had a message made of individual pieces of colored poster board, one or two letters per board, held end to end. When she finally got that one little boy to stand still, Annie got a good shot of the whole message held by all eight kids—the young ones squirming and grinning, the older kids looking like they'd rather be somewhere else:

ROOM ONE WELCOMES YOU!

Talking right into the camera, the teacher had said, "We're a very small school—only one room now, just nine kids in all. It was one of our students, Ted Hammond, the only sixth grader in town. He's the one who found the family staying in an empty farmhouse. And he took them food and supplies that he bought with his own money, and he's the one who's been trying to help them get their lives back on track. We're all proud that Ted's our friend."

Farther down Main Street, five veterans stood in a line in front of the American Legion Post wearing white shirts and blue caps with gold lettering. Annie got the camera in close on one man's face, weathered and wrinkled, and then slowly scanned down to the row of medals pinned on his shirt. This was great stuff.

When she heard a burst of applause from the far end of the street, Annie hurried to get her camera closer to the makeshift reviewing stand in front of the storefront with the sign that proclaimed PLATTSFORD TOWN HALL.

A buzz ran through the crowd—"That's them, that's the Hammonds' van."

A plain white Ford van had turned onto Main Street, the only vehicle in sight. And as it rolled along the street, the crowd whooped and cheered and clapped like mad.

The van came to a stop in front of the town hall, and Annie worked her way around to the passenger side. This was the big payoff, the moment she was waiting for. It was the moment the whole town was waiting for.

The passenger door opened, and a boy stood up on the running board, his head rising just a little above the roof of the van. The band stopped playing, the crowd hushed. Annie zoomed in for a tight shot of his face. She thought, *This must be the sixth grader.*

The boy looked around, and with a shy smile he said, "This is really incredible—it's . . . and thank you, all of you . . . and it's . . . well, they left. I talked to them this morning, and we had

planned to get them at four o'clock, but the family's gone. So . . . I'm sorry. But really, thanks . . . thanks."

Annie pulled the zoom lever, and her shot widened as the boy sat back down in the van and heaved the door shut. The driver, a woman, did a slow three-point turn, the brake lights winking on and off. And as the van drove away, Annie swung her camera back to the teacher and the kids, there next to the reviewing stand. Annie took a slow step or two closer so she'd get better sound, and through her earphones she heard the teacher say, "I know it's disappointing, but all this was still worth doing. When you try to do something kind, only good can come of it, no matter what. Now, I want you fourth graders to stay right here with me until your parents come. Kevin, come back here. Right here. No, *here*. Good."

Annie kept her camera running. The crowd started to break up, but she was surprised there wasn't more grumbling. It was like everyone had given one big shrug and then started talking with their friends. The legionnaires walked across Main Street toward the diner, the used-car dealer looked like he'd found a high-school boy who was interested in the bright red Dodge, the town manager folded up his reviewing stand—a card table with red, white, and blue crepe paper wrapped around its legs—and the Wheaton High School band began putting their instruments away and moving toward the big yellow bus parked on C Street. The excitement was over, and if there could have been a little more to the event, sure, that would have been good. But life in Plattsford was just settling back to normal, and that was okay too.

Annie couldn't wait to get home. She wanted to do a quick digital edit, and then upload some of this footage to her contact at KETV. Because with the right voice-over, this could be a sweet little story. Might even make the ten o'clock news.

But really, that didn't matter to her so much. Annie was just glad she'd been on hand to see this. For herself.

Chapter 27

HOMECOMING

The phone at the Hammond home had been ringing off the hook all evening.

The most interesting call came from an intern at the TV station in Omaha. He had to check on the spelling and pronunciation of about ten names. And he told Mrs. Hammond that the family ought to watch the ten o'clock news on KETV.

Most of the other calls had been from people around town, just wanting to have a word with Ted, wanting to thank him for trying to help that nice young family. After the tenth or twelfth call, Ted was pretty tired of hearing what a great job he'd done.

It wasn't the way he felt. First of all, April and her family had vanished. So how could that be good? And that giant scene on Main Street? Yes, he'd wanted the people in town to make the new family feel welcome, but he hadn't wanted a three-ring circus. He could only imagine how all the hoopla might have upset Alexa. The only part of that he'd asked for was the little banner that Mrs. Mitchell and the other kids from school had made, something simple.

By eight o'clock, Ted asked his mom to start telling people he had to do his homework. Which was true. But mostly, he needed to be alone.

About eight thirty, the phone rang again, and a minute later his mom brought the portable handset into his bedroom. She said, "Sorry, but you've got to take this one."

Ted took the phone and his mom slipped out the door.

"Hello?"

"Ted? It's me, April."

"April? Oh . . . well . . . hi." Then he said, "Where are you? Sounds loud."

"I'm in the back of my aunt's camper. We're almost to Colorado. And it's noisy because Artie's got his dumb Game Boy plugged in again."

"Oh." Ted didn't know what to say.

April said, "Sorry I didn't call you before

four o'clock, but my mom wouldn't let me—still kind of skittery. I felt bad, because I knew you'd be on time. But it's the best thing, I think, the way it happened. Artie and I told Mama about you and your mom comin' to help, and that she had to take it. The help. And it was like that woke her up or somethin'. She said, 'No, we've got relatives, and they're close enough so's we don't have to bother the people around here.' And that was it. We got out onto the highway round ten o'clock, and we got a ride to this truck stop about twenty miles west. Then Mama called her sister, and she hopped in her van to come get us. So we had to sit around that truck stop for five or six hours. But here we are. Aunt Rose is real nice. An' she says we can stay with her long as we need to."

Ted said, "I'm glad to hear that." And he was.

The line went quiet except for the highway noise and the beeps and whistles of a computer game. And then April said, "Hey, listen. If you ever get out by that farm again, the last one? I left somethin' there for you, under a board on the back steps. It's not much. But I hope you like it."

"Great," Ted said. "Thanks. I'll get it soon as I can. Tomorrow, prob'ly."

"Well, like I said, it's not much, not compared to what you did for us."

April tried to say something else, but there was static and skips in the signal.

"What?" said Ted. "Couldn't hear that."

"I said I've got to go—phone's cuttin' out."

Ted said, "Right—well, 'bye. And take care, okay? And come visit, if you want to."

"What?" April's voice was faint. "I'll . . ."

The line went dead.

On Friday morning Ted left enough time to swing past the Kosczinski farm before he delivered his papers. He rode into the drive, pedaled around to the back, and leaned his bike against the house.

And like April had said on the phone, there was a board with something tucked under it. It was wrapped with the same plastic he had used to cover *Little Women*. And the gift Ted unwrapped was another book, a cheap paperback that had been read so much that the pages looked puckered and worn out.

It was called *The Best of Sherlock Holmes*,

and on the inside front cover was a message, freshly written in dark blue ink.

For my friend
Ted Hammond,
from April Thayer
P.S. This is one of
my favorite books.
Do you like mysteries?

EPILOGUE

* * * ANCHOR DESK NOTES * * *

Thursday, May 27, Ten O'clock News,
KETV, Omaha

[cue camera 1: Anchor]

We've all heard of foster families, people who open their homes to help others in their time of need. But here's something new—a foster town, a whole town that was ready to reach out and adopt the bereaved family of a young soldier who died recently in Iraq.

[still photo: Corporal Austin Thayer]

Corporal Austin Thayer had been stationed outside of Baghdad to provide support for the recent elections, and he was killed when his armored unit came under attack.

[video: Main Street, Plattsford, NE]

This was the scene on Thursday afternoon as the whole town of Plattsford, Nebraska, turned out to welcome the wife and two children of a fallen First Cavalry soldier. A local boy had discovered the soldier's family living in an abandoned farmhouse. Here's what his teacher had to say today:

[cue video and sound: teacher interview]

"It was one of our students, Ted Hammond, the only sixth grader in town. He's the one who found the family staying in an empty farmhouse. And he took them food and supplies that he bought with his own money, and he's the one who's been trying to help them get their lives back on track. We're all proud that Ted's our friend."

[cue video, background sound: marching band, red car, diner]

People came from a fifty-mile radius today to show their support and love, serving up everything from automobiles . . . to fresh apple pie.

There was only one hitch in the festivities—

[cue video and sound: boy in van]

"This is really incredible—it's . . . and thank you, all of you . . . and it's . . . well, they left. I talked to them this morning, and we had planned to get them at four o'clock, but the family's gone. So . . . I'm sorry. But really, thanks . . . thanks."

[cue camera 1: Anchor]

That's right—the guests of honor, the soldier's wife, daughter, and son, decided at the last minute that they needed to move on and stay with relatives in Colorado. Even so, it was a grand gesture, right from the heartland, and right from the heart of the good people of Plattsford, Nebraska.

Casualty Assistance Center
Fort Hood, Texas

June 3

Master Theodore Hammond
175 Toronto Road
Plattsford, NE

Dear Ted:

When the Casualty Assistance Center here at Fort Hood learned from the Kansas State Police that a car registered to Corporal Austin Thayer had been found abandoned at a rest stop, we investigated. And when military police at Fort Hood discovered that Corporal Thayer's family had left town suddenly, you can imagine how concerned we became for their safety and well-being.

We have now heard from Corporal Thayer's wife, Alexa, who is staying with her sister in Colorado. We have also heard from her about the important part you played in helping her and her two children, April and Arthur, during their stay in your town.

On behalf of everyone here at the home of the First Cavalry, and particularly on behalf of the Casualty Assistance Center, I want to thank you. The army makes every effort to care for our soldiers and their family members. We are grateful to know that citizens like you are standing by, ready to help these good people whenever we cannot.

Again, thank you.

Sincerely,

MAJ. Leonard Parsten

Major Leonard Parsten
Casualty Assistance Calls Officer

FOSTER TOWN FOR MILITARY FAMILY

June 6, Plattsford, Nebraska (Associated Press)

THE PEOPLE OF PLATTSFORD, NEBRASKA, offered to become a foster town for the widow and children of a fallen soldier, and they made the offer out of the goodness of their hearts. Turns out they struck a chord in other hearts as well. Since the story first aired on May 27, the town offices report that inquiries and letters of thanks have been pouring in from across the country. The news has spread as far as Washington, D.C., where a broad coalition of congressional leaders plans to revisit the New Homestead Act, a law designed to encourage the repopulation of declining towns.

The army's Department of Casualty Assistance has also contacted the town of Plattsford to see if their offer holds good for other military families who might want to settle in a small town and start to rebuild their lives. And the answer is yes. The welcome mat is out for everyone.

So far more than two dozen bereaved military families have asked about the possibility of moving to this peaceful town on the Great Plains, and three families have already begun to make plans to move there during the summer. While there are not a lot of job prospects in Plattsford at the moment, the cost of housing is low, the community spirit is alive and well, and the town's one-room school is ready to grow, promising to provide an excellent education for children of all ages.

ACKNOWLEDGMENTS

I want to thank Mrs. Kim Metz at the Angora Public School in Angora, Nebraska, who shared her insights about the joys and problems of teaching in a one-room school.

Thanks also to Mr. Lee Price and the other kind people at the Casualty Assistance Center at Fort Hood, Texas, for helping me to be accurate and respectful in my brief portrayal of their difficult work.

This is a work of fiction, and I have made some purposeful mistakes in my storytelling that I hope will not offend the good people of Nebraska. For example, I know that the *Omaha Herald-Tribune* is not available for home delivery in the part of the state where my story is set. More significantly, while I have tried to stay true to some of the real-life challenges facing small towns with small schools, I have portrayed the process of Class I school affiliation and redistricting in Nebraska as far less complicated—and far less democratic—than it is in practice. For complete and factual information about Class I schools, please consult the Nebraska Department of Education Web site, http://www.nde.state.ne.us/.

HERE'S A LOOK AT

THE NEXT GREAT SCHOOL STORY FROM ANDREW CLEMENTS

CHAPTER 1

ZIPPED

Dave Packer was in the middle of his fourth hour of not talking. He was also in the middle of his social studies class on a Monday morning in the middle of November. And Laketon Elementary School was in the middle of a medium-size town in the middle of New Jersey.

There was a reason Dave was in the middle of his fourth hour of not talking, but this isn't the time to tell about that. This is the time to tell what he figured out in the middle of his social studies class.

Dave figured out that not talking is *extra* hard at school. And the reason? Teachers. Because at 11:35 Mrs. Overby clapped her hands and said, "Class—class! Quiet down!" Then she looked at her list and said, "Dave and Lynsey, you're next."

So Dave nodded at Lynsey and stood up. It was time to present their report about India.

But giving this report would ruin his experiment. Because Dave was trying to keep his mouth shut all day. He wanted to keep his lips zipped right up to the very end of the day, to not say one single word until the last bell rang at ten after three. And the reason Dave had decided to clam up . . . but it still isn't the time to tell about that. This is the time to tell what he did about the report.

Dave and Lynsey walked to the front of the room. Dave was supposed to begin the presentation by telling about the history of India. He looked down at his index cards, looked up at Mrs. Overby, looked out at the class, and he opened his mouth.

But he didn't talk.

He coughed. Dave coughed for about ten seconds. Then he wiped his mouth, looked at his index cards again, looked at Mrs. Overby again, looked at the class again, opened his mouth again, and . . . coughed some more. He coughed and coughed and coughed until his face was bright red and he was all bent over.

Lynsey stood there, feeling helpless. Dave hadn't told her about his experiment, so all she could do was watch—and listen to his horrible coughing. Lynsey's opinion of Dave had never been high, and it sank lower by the second.

Mrs. Overby thought she knew what was happening with Dave. She had seen this before—kids who got so nervous that they made themselves sick rather than talk in front of the class. It surprised her, because Dave wasn't shy at all. Ever. In fact, *none* of this year's fifth graders were the least bit shy or nervous about talking. Ever.

But the teacher took pity, and she said, "You'd better go get some water. You two can give your report later."

Lynsey gave Dave a disgusted look and went back to her desk.

Dave nodded at Mrs. Overby, coughed a few more times for good measure, and hurried out of the room.

And with Dave out in the hall getting a drink, it's the perfect time to tell why he was in the middle of his fourth hour of not talking, and why he had decided to keep quiet in the first place.

CHAPTER 2

GANDHI

When something happens, there's usually a simple explanation. But that simple explanation is almost never the full story.

Here's the simple explanation anyway: Dave had decided to stop talking for a whole day because of something he'd read in a book.

See? Very simple, very clear. But it's not the whole story.

So here's a little more.

Dave and a partner had to prepare a report on India—not a long one, just some basic facts. Something about the history, something about the government, something about the land and the industry, something about the Indian people and their culture. Five minutes or less.

Dave's report partner was Lynsey Burgess, and neither one of them was happy about that—there were some boy-girl problems at Laketon Elementary School. But this isn't the time to tell about that.

Even though Dave and Lynsey had to *give* their report together, they both agreed that they did *not* want to *prepare* it together. So they divided the topics in half, and each worked alone.

Dave was a good student, and he had found two books about India, and he had checked them out of the library. He hadn't read both books, not completely—he wasn't *that* good a student. But he had read parts of both books.

Dave thought the most interesting section in each book was the part about how India became independent, how the country broke away from England to become a free nation—sort of like the United States did.

And Dave thought the most interesting person in the story of India's independence was Mahatma Gandhi.

Dave was amazed by Gandhi. This one skinny little man practically pushed the whole British army out of India all by himself. But he didn't use weapons or violence. He fought with words and ideas. It was an incredible story, all of it true.

And in one of the books, Dave read this about Gandhi:

> For many years, one day each week Gandhi did not speak at all. Gandhi believed this was a way to bring order to his mind.

Dave read that bit of information on Thursday afternoon, and he read it again on Sunday night as he prepared for his oral report. And it made him wonder what that would be like—to go a whole day without saying a single word. And Dave began to wonder if not talking would bring order to *his* mind too.

In fact, Dave wondered what that meant, "to bring order to his mind." Could something as simple as not talking change the way your mind worked? Seemed like it must have been good for Gandhi. But what would it do for a regular kid in New Jersey?

Would not talking make him . . . smarter? Would he finally understand fractions? If he had more order in his mind, would he be able to look at a sentence and *see* which word was an adverb—instead of just guessing? And how about sports? Would someone with a more orderly mind be a better baseball player?

Powerful questions.

So Dave decided to zip his lip and give it a try.

Was it hard for him to keep quiet? You bet, especially at first, like when he got to the bus stop, where his friends were arguing about why the Jets had lost to the Patriots. But Dave had learned quickly that by nodding and smiling, by frowning and shrugging, by shaking his head, by giving a thumbs-up or a high five, or even by just putting his hands in his coat pockets and turning away, not talking was possible. And by the time he'd ridden the bus to school, Dave had gotten pretty good at fitting in without speaking up.

There. That explains what's going on a little better. And it's probably enough, at least for the moment. But there's more. There's *always* more.

And now we're back in class on Monday with Dave, who got through the rest of social studies without saying a word. And when the bell rang at the end of the period, it was time for fifth-grade lunch.

More than a hundred and twenty-five kids began hurrying toward the cafeteria. And by the time they got there, the fifth graders were already talking like crazy—all except one.

CHAPTER 3

INSULTS

"If you had to shut up for five minutes, I bet the whole top of your head would explode!" As those words flew out of his mouth, Dave had two thoughts.

First, he thought, *Darn it!*—because he remembered he'd been trying not to talk at all.

And his second thought was, *Gandhi probably wouldn't have said that.* Because it wasn't a very nice thing to say.

But that's what Dave said, and he said it to Lynsey Burgess, and there was a reason he said it.

So it's time to back up a little and explain.

Dave had gotten through the lunch line without a peep. He had pointed at the pizza plate, then pointed at the fruit cup. He had nodded for "yes, please" and shook his head for "no, thanks." He had grabbed some milk from the cooler and flashed his lunch pass at Mrs. Vitelli. And he had smiled a lot.

No talking? No problem.

Then he'd sat down at a table with some of his friends, just like always. But instead of jumping into the conversation, Dave had kept a pleasant look on his face, and he'd kept his mouth full of food.

No talking? No problem.

And because he wasn't talking, Dave had focused all his energy on listening.

Listening at the lunch table, really *listening*, was a brand-new experience for him. Because most of the time Dave was a loudmouth.

See? There's something more about Dave. And it makes Dave's reaction to Gandhi make more sense. Because if Dave himself was a loudmouth, a real tongue-flapper, then someone like Gandhi who could keep completely quiet would seem that much more amazing.

Because Dave really did love to talk. He could talk and talk and talk about almost anything—baseball, cars, dinosaurs, rock hunting, soccer, snowboarding, waterskiing, favorite books, best football players, camping, canoeing, PlayStation, Nintendo, Xbox, comic books, TV shows, movies—you name it. Dave had a long, long list of interests, and he had plenty of opinions.

Plus, talking always made Dave feel like he was in charge. It was sort of like being a police officer out in the middle of traffic. As long as *he* did the talking, the traffic went the way *he* wanted it to. This was especially useful if insults started flying around. When it came to dishing out the put-downs, Dave was a pro.

But this lunchtime, all the *other* loudmouths were getting a chance to spout off.

So Dave had chewed his pizza, and sipped his milk, and listened. And after a minute or two he began listening to Lynsey Burgess. But only because he couldn't help it.

Even though she was sitting behind him at the next table, and even though the cafeteria was almost bursting with noise, Lynsey had a sharp voice, the kind that cuts like a hacksaw.

". . . so I said, 'Are you serious?' and she said, 'What's wrong with you?' and I said, 'Because I saw it first,' and I did, and it was a great color for me, because my hair's brown, and her hair's that mousy blond color, but her mom was right there in the store, so she picked it up and took it over to her, and her mom bought it! Can you *believe* that? She *knew* I wanted that sweater more than anything, and she bought it anyway. And then? After school on Friday at soccer practice? She *smiled* at me, like she wanted to be friends or something—as *if*! Can you *believe* that?"

No, Dave couldn't believe it. He couldn't believe that anyone could flap and yap her mouth so fast, and say so many words, and be so boring and stupid-sounding, all at the same time. He took another bite of pizza and tried to stop listening, but Lynsey was just getting warmed up.

". . . because then, she comes over *after* practice? And she says, 'Here, this is for you,' and she tries to *give* me the sweater. So I pull my hands away like she's holding a dead skunk or something, and I say, 'You think I want *that*? That thing is so ugly, I would *never* wear that!' And she says, 'Oh'—just like that—just, 'Oh'—and she walks away with the sweater. Except now, I wish I hadn't said that, because it really is the *best* color, and it's really soft. . . ."

By this point, Dave was wishing he had an iPod. Because if he had one, and if it hadn't been against school rules, he could have plugged up both his ears and cranked the volume. Anything to get away from the sound of Lynsey's voice.

"... because once I tried wearing this sweater that was made of wool? And it made my neck itch *so* much, like, I couldn't even wear it for two minutes, but it was okay, because then my mom found this turtleneck way down in the bottom of my dresser, and I'd forgotten I even had it, and it was pink, so then I put that on first, and then the sweater was fine, because, really, it was like the two colors went together *perfectly*, almost like a picture in a magazine. Because last week in *Teen People*? Jenna and Lori and Keith were at this party, like, in Hollywood or somewhere? And Jenna had on a sweater that was almost like that wool one I have, and she was wearing these . . ."

And that was the moment when Dave completely forgot about keeping silent, and he turned around and almost shouted, "If you had to shut up for five minutes, I bet the whole top of your head would explode!"

And Dave was glad he'd said it, even if it wasn't nice, and even though it ended his experiment. Because after he said it, Lynsey stopped talking.

But the quiet only lasted about three seconds.

Lynsey said, "Is your *cough* all better? Because I

thought I just heard a whiny little voice." She and her friends stared at Dave. "Did you say something?"

"Yeah, I did," he said. "I *said*, I bet if you had to shut up for five minutes, the top of your head would explode. Like a volcano. From all the hot gas that usually comes out of your mouth. When you talk and talk and talk and never stop talking. Yeah. That's what I said. To you."

Lynsey tilted her head and looked at Dave, sort of the way a bird looks at a bug it's about to eat.

"Oh, like there's something *wrong* with talking? You never have any trouble with *yourself* blabbing and blabbing every day. We've all *heard* you." And the other girls nodded and made faces.

"Well," Dave said, "talking's okay, when there's stuff worth saying."

Lynsey said, "*Ohhh*—so *boys* can say things like, 'Hey, did you hear this guy got traded to that team, and that guy got traded to this team, and, hey, he hit real good last year, and, ooh yeah, he can really catch!' Boys can talk and talk like that, but girls can't talk about clothes sometimes? Is *that* it?"

Dave said, "No . . . but I don't talk the way you talk, like, for a million minutes in a row without stopping. And . . . and . . ."

Dave was hunting for something strong to say, a real punch line, something that would shut Lynsey up and end this conversation. So he said, ". . . and anyway, boys *never* talk as much as girls do, ever!"

Please take a careful look at that last thing Dave just said.

Because with this particular group of fifth graders, *that* was a dangerous thing to say.

And now is a good time to tell a little more about the fifth-grade boys and the fifth-grade girls at Laketon Elementary School—to explain why it was a bad idea for Dave to say what he just said.

Because Dave should have kept his mouth shut.

He really should have.